Books by Dale Hartley Emery

Science Fiction and Fantasy

Carrion Road

Funhouse

Refund

Tailor's Tears

Yantriel's Privy

Collections

Winding Unwinding

For more information about these books
and other fine fiction from Driscoll Brook Press,
visit www.DriscollBrookPress.com

WINDING
UNWINDING

DALE HARTLEY EMERY

DRISCOLL
BROOK
PRESS

Winding Unwinding

Published by Driscoll Brook Press
www.DriscollBrookPress.com

© 2014 by Dale Hartley Emery
Cover design © 2014 by Driscoll Brook Press
Cover art © Annnmei | Dreamstime.com

ISBN: 978-1-63261-010-2

This is a work of fiction. Names, characters, businesses, places, events and incidents are either the products of the author's imagination or used in a fictitious manner. Any resemblance to actual persons, living or dead, or actual events is purely coincidental.

For Lisa,
who supplies
all the magic
I will ever need

WINDING
UNWINDING

Contents

INTRODUCTION

M ANY YEARS AGO, I read *Danse Macabre*, Stephen King's non-fiction book about horror and fantasy fiction. In the middle of the book, King says:

Fantasy fiction is essentially about the concept of power

That one line was a major insight for me. I suddenly understood why I am so attracted to fantasy stories: I am fascinated by power.

And King's line also explained why I write fantasy stories: I write fantasy in order to explore power.

Of course, it is not only fantasy stories that are about power. Most stories in any genre are about power in one way or another.

But fantasy puts power front and center. Fantasy hinges on magic, and magic is power, concentrated and inexplicable.

A confession: Writing fantasy allows me to cheat. It unbinds me from the constraints of the laws of physics, and lets me aim my fiction right at the heart of power. Power that is unattainable in the real world. Power that is exaggerated so that it is easier to observe and impossible to avoid.

As much as I enjoy entertaining people with my fiction, ultimately I write fantasy to explore my own questions about power. What are our fears and fantasies about power? How do we learn to accept the power we have? How do we cope when we discover that our power has unexpected consequences, good and bad, small and large? What responsibility do we have for using our power, even knowing deep down that the effects are not entirely within our control?

Mind you, I don't have any answers for these questions. But I have great fun forcing my fictional characters to struggle with them.

The five stories in *Winding Unwinding* are contemporary fantasy, each taking place in a world more or less like our own.

In "Tailor's Tears," Clarke Whiteley learns that his own aura magic is only one of the forces unwinding his life, and perhaps not the most powerful force.

In "Carrion Road," Carla discovers that the two people with whom she hitched a ride have a strange power over the road. But even their power is limited.

In "Funhouse," Mark and Davy find that even intelligence (an inexplicable magic if ever there was one) may not be powerful to get them out of the funhouse alive.

In "Refund," Geoff Palmenter receives an inexplicable and powerful gift of time. But even magical time is fleeting.

In "Yantriel's Privy," a humble farmer finds himself battling swarms of frogs. Frogs that wield a disturbing power.

Magic. Inexplicable power. In each story, an inexplicable power winds tighter and tighter. In each story, the characters struggle to keep the power from unwinding their lives. Winding. Unwinding.

I have added an author's note after each story. If you're interested in how the stories came to be, read those. But read the story first.

I hope you enjoy reading these stories. I certainly enjoyed writing them.

There will be more.

Dale Hartley Emery
Sacramento, California
August 3, 2014

TAILOR'S TEARS

1. A Tattered Wedding Dress

THERE ARE THREE THINGS a tailor needs above all others: cloth, needles, and a fresh supply of tears. Clarke Whiteley was all out of tears. He looked at Dulcie Byers's wedding dress, in tatters on the cutting table, and wondered whether he could retire on the money in his savings account. He decided he could not.

Clarke's workshop was empty now, his boutique closed. The cheap battery-powered wall clock ticked heavily, and the mid-afternoon humidity hung in the room like a gas leak.

Dulcie Byers was likely halfway home by now, screaming into her cell phone at her unworthy fiancé that the tailor he recommended, the tailor he *insisted* that she use, had ruined her $3,000 wedding dress. Maybe she would scream, as she had at Clarke, that he had ruined her life.

She had a point.

Hue Hawthorne, the unworthy fiancé, would call Clarke to find out what had happened, to find out how to make this right. That conversation would lead to nowhere, and he too would yell at Clarke, about trust, about putting my faith in you, about third and fourth chances, about I knew you would let me down when it really mattered.

Ten years earlier Clarke had shepherded Hue through his senior year at Brown University, tutoring, writing papers, stealing advance copies of upcoming tests, ensuring Professor Combover that surely he was mistaken, surely it was not Hue Hawthorne he had spotted with tender young Fiona Combover leaving Rosa's Ristorante, because on Thursday evening Hue had been in the library with Clarke, studying diligently for the poli-sci midterm.

Hue was nothing if not grateful, but gratitude had a shelf life. The cheesy clock on Clarke's wall ticked past the expiration date.

The boutique's phone rang, and Clarke answered before the first ring died away. "Hey, Hue."

"You son of a cur. What have you done to my daughter-in-law?" It was not Hue. It was the elder Hawthorne. Assemblyman Gorance Goldsmith Hawthorne III. Old Gory had never liked Clarke.

"I'm sure she's told you the whole story herself," Clarke said, sure she had done no such thing.

"The poor girl was unconsolable. Incoherent. Couldn't say three words without breaking into great gasping sobs. How could you let her drive in that state?"

That had been a mistake. It would also have been a mistake to try to reason with an enraged bride-to-be in a room full of scissors.

"I do hope she gets home safely."

Gory shouted, "You do not want to play games with me, you little weasel. I advise you to repair that dress with all possible haste."

"That won't be possible—"

"Why not? What sort of incompetent tailor are you?"

"I am competent. I am not magical." Which was exactly the opposite of the truth. And that was what created this whole mess. He should not have imbued Hue's fiancée's wedding dress with magic. Not with a maiden aura. Not four days before the wedding.

And certainly not without conferring with the bride.

"Is it money? Is that it? Four days before the wedding and you stoop to extortion?"

"No, sir, nothing like that," Clarke said. "I can't repair it for any amount of money. It's been torn to shreds." And imbued to glow with the subtle pink aura of virginity at her moment of happiness.

Assuming she was actually a virgin.

Gory screamed, "Why in the name of all the gods would you do such a thing?"

"Actually, Mister Hawthorne, she was the one who—"

"'He ruined it.' Those were the three words she was able to choke out between sobs. 'He ruined it.'"

Clarke had to admit that she was right. Sure, she was the one who had torn the dress to shreds, but by then it was already ruined.

"I assure you it was an accident." Not so much an accident as an oversight. He should have known better than to take the prospective mother-in-law's word for something as potentially catastrophic as this. Even if she was the wife of the most powerful politician in the county. Especially then.

"Well, for god's sake, man, make it right." Gory's voice no longer sounded angry. More like pleading.

Make it right. It sounded like such a reasonable plea. "I will do what I can, Mister Hawthorne," Clarke said. "I promise—"

"You would be surprised how little I value your promises right now," Hawthorne said, and Clarke could just picture the man spitting the words through clenched teeth. "But do make this right. I am feeling an exaggerated sense of stress in my life right now, and I would not want that to affect my professional judgment in the upcoming zoning board meetings. A happy, boring wedding would be a great relief. Am I making myself clear?"

Clarke's Corner Clothier was on the western edge of the commercial zone, next to a large undeveloped lot. Hawthorne was golf buddies with Mathias McCoy, the owner of the lot, who wanted to expand his holdings eastward and build an apartment complex or a strip mall or a putt putt golf course. The five-year zoning plan was up for review next month. The chairman of the assembly's zoning committee was none other than Gorance Goldsmith Hawthorne III.

Yes, Gory was making himself clear. Clarke bristled at the threat. Gory could have appealed to Clarke's human decency. Or to his sense of business propriety. Or even to guilt. The implication that Clarke would do the right thing only under threat was an insult.

But not entirely undeserved.

Clarke said, "I think we're all hoping for a happy wedding, sir."

Gory was right. Clarke had to make this right.

He had no idea how he was going to do that. But it had to start with Dulcie.

2. A BRIDE'S REQUEST

CLARKE CALLED DULCIE the next morning. To his surprise, she agreed to meet with him. To his greater surprise, she insisted they meet at his boutique. He would not have thought she would be willing to visit again so soon after yesterday's conversation, which had humiliated Dulcie and mortified Clarke. But she wanted to meet in absolute privacy. Clarke could understand that.

On the phone she seemed surprisingly amenable to working things out, but Clarke took the precaution of locking the workshop and arranging to meet in his office.

At noon Clarke posted a handwritten "closed for lunch" sign on the glass door. Five minutes later, Dulcie arrived, wearing a Carl Perkins T-shirt, black jeans, and blue suede shoes.

He opened the door, and the breeze jingled the door chimes. Her gentle scent caught him by surprise, and he rocked on his heels for a moment. She always smelled lovely, but something was different today.

"I'm glad you called, Clarke," she said. "I'm sorry for the way I acted yesterday. And for anything Hue's dad might have said." She smiled and held out her hand.

Clarke took her hand, small and soft and warm. She held his gaze for a moment, and when he released her hand, she blushed and looked away.

Clarke led Dulcie to his office. On the walls, models of all ages and colors smiled and pouted in their elegant jackets and dresses. Below the photos, fashion magazines lay on catalogue racks in which catalogs leaned on each other.

Clarke took the seat behind his desk, and Dulcie the one in front.

"I never noticed that before," Dulcie said, pointing over Clarke's shoulder.

A plaque hung there, announcing that Clarke's Corner Clothier was a member of the Chamber of Commerce. It was signed by Gorance Goldsmith Hawthorne III.

Clarke said, "I suppose he regrets signing that right now."

"Let me know if he gives you any trouble over this." Dulcie looked down at her folded hands. "I realize that Helen Ruth put you up to this. She can be very persuasive. You wouldn't have had any reason to doubt her."

Clarke touched the fingertips of both hands to his chest. "Miss Byers, I take total responsibility. I violated not only the Code of— well, the code of good business conduct. I also violated my own good judgment."

Dulcie leaned forward and smiled. "Do you magicians have a code?"

A code of ethics. And a code of secrecy. Clarke did not know how Helen Ruth Hawthorne learned of his unadvertised skills, and she refused to tell him. But it was a reliable source, she had said. And several people in "the inner circle" would be in attendance at the wedding. She did not say what inner circle.

"It's not something I am supposed to talk about."

Dulcie sat up straight. "Then let's get down to business. I am in need of a wedding dress. And the need is rather urgent."

Clarke laughed and nodded. "I have good news and bad news. The good news is that I was able to clear my calendar for the rest of the week. I'm sure I can reproduce the pattern from Mrs. Hawthorne's, uh, the pattern I used before. Probably by Friday noon. Assuming that's what you want."

"Oh, yes," Dulcie said. "Helen Ruth's wedding dress was gorgeous. I may be furious at her, but that's no reason for me to settle for second best."

"That brings me to the bad news. I'm afraid I can't get the organza in time. I called Teobaldo in Vicenza this morning, and the earliest they could possibly ship is Friday. Then there's no way I could finish the dress in time for the wedding on Saturday, much less in time for a fitting and adjustments."

"Oh," Dulcie said, her shoulders sagging. "That is bad news."

"But we can buy very fine organza at any number of shops here in Portsmouth or Kittery."

"Helen Ruth's fabric came from Vicenza."

"I'm sorry."

The muscles in Dulcie's jaw bunched. Through clenched teeth she said, barely above a whisper, "If my fabric is second best, how can I top Helen Ruth's dress?"

The sudden bite of Dulcie's competitiveness surprised Clarke into silence for a moment. When Dulcie and Helen Ruth had walked into Clarke's shop arm-in-arm all those months ago, they had instructed Clarke to duplicate Helen Ruth's dress as closely as possible. Helen Ruth had supplied the original pattern, which Clarke would have to adjust for Dulcie, who was nearly a foot shorter than she. And Helen Ruth had supplied the address of the same Italian weaver who had made her organza. "I do regret, Dulcie dear, that I can't give you my actual wedding dress," Helen Ruth had said. "Alas, it was destroyed in an attic fire. The charred bits crumbled in my hands as I wept."

Had Dulcie's competitive streak been there all along? Clarke had not noticed it before, but weddings often brought latent family tensions bubbling to the surface, and Clarke had trained himself not to notice the bubbles.

"I'm sorry," Clarke said again.

"Could we..." Dulcie nodded toward the wall that separated Clarke's office from the workshop.

"No, no," Clarke said. "There are really no pieces left to work with. I'm—" He stopped himself from repeating that he was sorry.

Dulcie's chin quivered for a moment. Clarke was about to reach for a tissue when she said, "I guess second best will have to do."

Clarke said, "It won't be second best. Not with you in it." Whoops. That was over the line.

Dulcie sniffled, then smiled. "That's sweet." She leaned forward, touched his hand gently, and stood up. "But you know, Clarke, you're right. If this dress is half as lovely as the first one you made for me, I will be a beautiful bride."

Relieved, Clarke escorted Dulcie to the door. She thanked him again, and swept out the door. It looked as if everything were going to turn out just fine.

Clarke was still standing with his hand on the closed door when Dulcie came skipping back and tapped on the glass.

When he opened the door, she was bouncing up and down on the balls of her feet.

"I just had the most brilliant idea. Clarke, I think I know where I can get the perfect organza. Can you wait until tomorrow morning to start on the dress?"

He might have to work late for a few days, but he was sure he could do it. "I'll need it by noon at the latest."

"That's marvelous, Clarke," Dulcie said. She stood on tiptoes and kissed him on the cheek. Then she bounded down the street.

3. A Virgin's Tears

ON WEDNESDAY AT ONE PM Dulcie called to say she would need more time to locate the organza, but she expected to have it in a few hours. Three and a half hours later she still had not found the fabric, but said there were only a few more places to look. Clarke mentally inventoried the nearby shops that sold decent fabric. By now she would have exhausted every shop in seacoast New Hampshire and would be venturing into southern Maine. Clarke offered again to purchase the organza himself, but Dulcie said no, she knew exactly what she was looking for.

At ten a.m. on Thursday, Dulcie called again and breathlessly announced that she had found it. The perfect organza. She would bring it soon, but she needed a while longer to prepare it.

Before Clarke could ask her what she meant by "prepare," she hung up.

Dulcie arrived a little after noon carrying a large shopping bag. By this time, Clarke had counted and recounted the remaining hours before the wedding. It was less than two days away. If everything went well, he would be able to finish the dress by late Friday. And even if everything went well, that left no time for alterations.

He should not have waited for Dulcie to find the "perfect" organza. He should have implemented a backup plan. He should have bought a supply of fabric himself and started on the dress, just in case.

But it was too late for that now.

Dulcie laid the shopping bag on the counter and grinned at Clarke. "The perfect organza," she said. "Take a look."

Clarke peeked in the bag and was puzzled. He expected to see one or two large swaths of fabric. Instead he saw dozens of pieces of all shapes and sizes.

Dulcie said, "And it's Italian."

Clarke reached into the bag and took a piece of the fabric in his fingers, a sinking feeling growing in his stomach. He held up the piece. Clarke recognized the shape. It exactly matched one of the shoulder pieces from Helen Ruth Hawthorne's pattern.

"From Vicenza."

Clarke now understood what Dulcie had meant by "prepare." She had removed the stitches from Helen Ruth's wedding dress and reduced it to pieces.

"Dulcie, you didn't."

"I did," Dulcie said.

"Did Helen Ruth give you this?"

"Of course. You heard her when we first came here. 'I do wish, dear, that I could give you my own wedding dress.'"

That was not at all the same thing as actually giving Dulcie the dress. Helen Ruth claimed that the dress was destroyed. That was clearly a lie. She clearly did not want Dulcie to have this dress.

Clarke stuffed the shoulder piece back in the bag and set the bag upright. "Dulcie, I can't use this."

Slowly, Dulcie said, "She owes me a wedding dress."

"You can't just steal her wedding dress." Clarke lifted the bag and headed for the door, as if getting the thing out of his shop would somehow make everything good again. "And I can't use stolen cloth."

Dulcie stepped in front of Clarke, blocking his path. "You and Helen Ruth destroyed my wedding dress. You owe me. Both of you."

She had a point. If it had not been for Helen Ruth's meddling and his irresponsibility, Dulcie would have her dress by now.

But still. "Dulcie, I can't—"

She laid a hand softly on his cheek. "You owe me, Clarke."

He wished she would stop saying that. But she was right. He did owe her. And Helen Ruth had meddled. And Gory was the head of the zoning board. And Clarke was out of time.

He looked at the bag of expensive scraps of Helen Ruth Hawthorne's wedding dress. He closed his eyes and nodded.

"It's settled, then," Dulcie said.

Clarke motioned toward the door. "I should get started, then."

"Clarke..." Dulcie bit the tip of a fingernail and smiled coyly. "I have a favor to ask." As if using the organza ripped from her mother-in-law's stolen wedding dress were not favor enough. "I've been thinking. If it's not too late, I would like the maiden aura after all."

"What? But I thought you—" Clarke blinked and caught himself before he finished the sentence: I thought you were not a virgin.

"Yes, I was terribly upset at Helen Ruth's being so presumptuous. An aura is such a personal thing. But now I think it might be fun. A little surprise for Hue. He has been very patient with me." Dulcie frowned. "Wait. You thought I what?"

"Nothing, nothing. It's just that you were so upset on Monday."

She smiled again. "Monday was Monday, and today is today. This is my only wedding. I may as well have some fun. Can you do it?"

"I'm afraid I can't. I'm all out of tailor's tears."

"What's that? Like eye of newt?"

"Tears from a virgin bride. I ordered some, but the shipment won't come for a week or two. I guess they're very hard to come by."

Dulcie laughed. "Are virgin brides so rare?"

"It's more the verification procedure."

"Oh," she said, the hollows of her neck turning pink.

"We have to be absolutely certain, otherwise the effects—" Clarke shook his head. "Weddings have been ruined."

Dulcie waggled a finger at her eyes. "How much do you need?"

Clarke hesitated. It was risky to imbue an aura for someone using their own tears. Sometimes the magic and the target amplified something in each other, or canceled something out. The effect was usually the desired one, but it might be amplified or dampened, or it might oscillate. "Dulcie, I don't think this is a good—"

She put her hands on her hips, elbows out. "How much do you need?"

The bigger risk was using tears from someone other than a virgin. The effects were unpredictable. Something in the tears would interact with something in the target, and something would happen. Usually something interesting.

But he couldn't raise that subject again. Instead he said, "I'm really not supposed to use a person's tears for their own aura. The results are—"

Dulcie, hands still on hips, elbows still pointing menacingly outward, stuck her chin forward. "How much, Clarke?"

Clarke wanted to object, wanted to give a stronger warning, wanted to at least ask if she were really, really sure she wanted to do this. But wasn't she already insisting? Didn't that mean she was a virgin? He was almost certain.

Almost.

But to ask was to insult. And insult, he decided, was the greatest risk of all.

Clarke sighed. "I need a few cc's."

Dulcie nodded. "Do you have something I can cry into?"

He directed her to the bathroom, a vial and a tiny paper funnel in her hand. When she emerged, the vial was half full, and both of her eyes were puffy and red.

"Thank you for doing this," she said, handing him the vial. Then she smiled just the way she had the day before.

He smiled in return, thinking about the way she had raised herself up on tiptoes to kiss him on the cheek.

But she did not kiss him today. She blushed and looked away, then turned and walked out the door.

Clarke tucked the vial in his pocket and gathered up Helen Ruth's hand-woven Italian organza.

As he shuffled into the workshop to begin work on the dress, his insides twisted into a writhing knot, he fully intended to imbue the dress with a maiden aura made from Dulcie's own tears.

4. A Perfect June Day

IT WAS THE PERFECT JUNE DAY for a wedding.

Clarke had visited the Hawthornes' mansion only once, and then only long enough to pick up Hue after a weekend visit and drive south to Brown. He had never seen the back yard.

The lawn rolled gently eastward over irregular hillocks for a hundred yards before it met a forest of oak and pine and birch. Four flower gardens vaguely marked one edge of the lawn. A long hedge marked another. In the middle of the lawn a large tent shaded a dozens of tables covered in powder blue tablecloths.

Family and friends milled about near the house, around a huge flagstone patio lined with scores of white wooden folding chairs, each with a thin powder blue cushion. Beside the patio, parasols shaded two men and two women, each dressed in a tuxedo, as they tuned their violins and violas and cellos.

Wispy clouds threw intermittent shade. A warm breeze blew from the east, carrying the smells of ocean and pine.

The string quartet began playing a lush, languorous tune, the signal for the guests to be seated. Clarke took a seat at the back.

At either end of the patio a sliding glass door led into the house. Every few moments, some member of the wedding party would open one of the doors, peek out and scan the guests, then pop back into the house and slide the door closed.

The quartet finished the slow song and began a more playful one. From the door on the left, Gory and Helen Ruth Hawthorne emerged and walked slowly to two empty seats, front and center. As they sat, a man seated behind Helen Ruth tapped her on the shoulder. She turned, and the man handed her a small box, about a foot long and three inches wide, made of dark wood. The box seemed to have designs carved into the sides, though at this distance Clarke could not tell what they were.

As Helen Ruth faced front, the man glanced furtively to the left, then to the right. Clarke had seen the man before, but could not remember where or when. An image began to form in Clarke's mind.

The sliding glass doors opened. Barbara Emmons, the Methodist pastor, stepped out, wearing a long ivory robe and long red stole. Two young men in perfect tuxedos followed Pastor Emmons. They looked like twins, their features similar to Hue's and Gory's. Probably cousins of Hue.

From the door on the right came two young women dressed in long powder blue dresses. The pastor walked to the front of the patio, and the twin groomsmen and the bridesmaids took their positions several paces to either side of her.

Inside the house a woman burst into laughter, then suddenly stopped, as if she (or someone) had clamped a hand over her mouth. The groomsmen and bridesmaids looked at each other with raised eyebrows and laughed.

A man about Clarke's age stepped through the groom's door, followed by Hue. They took up positions between the groomsmen and bridesmaids, Hue licking his lips and clearing his throat every few seconds.

A woman stepped through the bride's door, her eyes crinkling with suppressed laughter, the sides of her neck flushing pink. She walked to Hue and whispered something. Hue shook his head, grinned, and looked at his feet.

The music grew louder.

Hue turned and glanced at his mother. Then he looked beyond her and his eyes widened.

That's when Clarke realized where he had seen the man behind Helen Ruth. It was the political science professor from Brown University, Professor Combover. He was wearing a toupee now. And his hair was black instead of the mousy brown it had been.

What was his real name? Some of the students had another nickname for him. It was on the tip of Clarke's tongue. Bernie Baldie. That was it. His name was Bernard Theobald.

Clarke felt a sudden dread.

Theobald. Teobaldo. The same name as Helen Ruth's weavers in Vicenza.

And then he knew what was in the dark wooden box that Bernard Theobald had handed to Helen Ruth. It was the shuttle that the Teobaldo weavers had used to weave the organza.

A weaver's wand.

A weaver's tools retained a subtle link to any cloth they helped to make. A skilled weaver who was also skilled in the subtle arts could imbue a shuttle with subtle power. Under the right conditions, the shuttle could be used to distort any magic embedded in the items made from the cloth.

It was the same for any hand-crafted items made from hand-crafted materials. The guilds vetted all apprentices to ensure that "only the right kind of people" gained access to the subtle arts. And they instilled and enforced a code of ethics to, among other things, prevent the handful of magical artisans of one craft from identifying the handful of magical artisans of another.

Breaches of the code were exceedingly rare. Every one was infamous. Not one ended happily.

There was only one reason Helen Ruth would be holding the weaver's wand for her son's bride's wedding dress. She intended mischief.

A wave of mixed horror and relief passed through Clarke. He had nearly done as Dulcie had asked. He nearly imbued her dress with a maiden aura catalyzed by her own tears. Alone in his workshop on Friday, he held an eyedropper full of Dulcie's tears in mid-air, and let a single drop fall onto the dress, at the top the left shoulder. Then he hesitated. Doubt overcame him. Overwhelmed him. Aura magic was subtle, too delicate to trifle with, especially for an occasion as momentous as a wedding. Using Dulcie's own tears was just too risky. And he had not promised. Not in so many words. But that was just rationalizing, he knew. Dulcie would be furious at him, and she had every right to be. But in the end, he made his choice. He would prefer her fury at what he had not done to the disaster that he might cause if his magic were to go awry.

At this moment, as he watched Helen Ruth rub a long-nailed thumb up and down the worn edge of the weaver's wand, he felt great relief that he had listened to his doubts.

Clarke had averted disaster. He did not expect that Dulcie would be placated by that explanation, but that no longer mattered. What mattered was that he had saved her wedding from certain catastrophe.

The quartet stopped the playful song mid-beat, paused for a second, then began "The Wedding March." Everyone rose to their feet. Someone in the front said, "Ooh," then another, then another.

Dulcie Byers emerged from the bride's door on the arm of Eldon Byers, her father. In the dress that Clarke had made from Helen Ruth's organza, she looked gorgeous. Dulcie stepped into the warm breeze, the dress flowing gently around her legs.

As Dulcie passed the bridesmaids, she glanced sideways toward Helen Ruth and raised an eyebrow. One corner of her mouth turned slightly upward.

Helen Ruth smiled bitterly in return.

Gorance Hawthorne looked from one to the other and frowned.

Dulcie stepped into place beside Hue. He smiled adoringly at her and took her hand.

As the guests sat, Helen Ruth turned and glared at Clarke. She mouthed the word, "Now."

Clarke smiled at her. In a moment she would discover that her plans had been foiled.

Someone in the crowd gasped.

On the patio, Hue took a step back, his jaw dropping.

Dulcie's dress was ever so slightly pink.

At first, Clarke thought the coloring was a trick of the light, a bit of fantasy of what he wished he could have done for Dulcie.

He held a hand over his eyes and squinted. No, this was not a trick of the light. The dress was pink, all right, and the color was deepening.

This could not be.

Dulcie glanced down, then at Hue, her smile filled with both pride and bliss.

Had Theobald placed a maiden aura on Helen Ruth's dress while it was in the attic? That didn't make sense. Neither he nor Helen Ruth would have been able to guess that Dulcie would even find the dress, much less steal the cloth for her own dress.

If this were a maiden aura, Dulcie would have a modicum of control over the strength of the effect. All you had to do to control an aura was concentrate on the appropriate quality inside yourself. But fine control took a bit of practice, and Dulcie had had none. Clarke expected the effect to fluctuate.

It did not.

Dulcie's dress flared neon pink, then dull pink, then red. The veil pulsed orange, then white, then pink.

Hue's eyes went wide in confusion as he watched his bride's dress jump randomly from color to color.

This was not a maiden aura after all. It was something else. Something that caused a color burst.

Clarke breathed a sigh of relief. A color burst was minor magic. Amateur artists used it to impress their small-town friends.

Spectacular but harmless. This could have been so much worse.

But Dulcie probably did not know it was harmless. She looked down at the dress, a look of horror deepening on her face. She turned toward Clarke.

Clarke could not meet her gaze. He looked away, and there was Helen Ruth. She nodded toward him, her eyes twinkling, a self-satisfied smile on her face.

Someone screamed, then everyone was shouting and pointing and looking about.

Then the dress and veil turned gray, and one gigot shoulder fell away.

The shoulder on which Clarke had dropped the one teardrop.

Dulcie watched, mannequin-still, as the fabric slid down her arm and onto the flagstones.

Yes, a disintegrating wedding dress was worse.

And Clarke knew that he could not predict how much worse it would get.

"Dulcie!" he cried at the top of his lungs.

She turned to look at him, her hands held out to her sides, her mouth forming a mute O, and he realized he had not expected to actually get her attention. He had no idea what to say.

And yet he was still yelling. "Get out of the dress. Take it off now!"

Incomprehensibly, everyone went quiet and turned toward Clarke. The photographer swung his camera around to point at Clarke.

Hue said, "Whiteley?"

Dulcie stood very still, her face bunching, her eyes filling with tears.

Clarke could not think of what to say to snap her out of her shock, to get her out of her dress.

But he had to get her out of that dress.

With everyone turned accusingly toward Clarke, the narrow center aisle between the folding chairs was unobstructed. There was nothing between Clarke and Dulcie.

He ran toward her, sending Hue and Dulcie's friends and relatives jerking back in surprise.

Helen Ruth placed her hands on Theobald's back and shoved. He stumbled into the aisle, hands pinwheeling to the sides for balance.

Unable to avoid the collision, Clarke lowered his shoulder and hit Theobald in chest, resulting in a sickening oof like someone coughing up a hunk of steak.

Theobald's feet flew forward and his head snapped back, his toupee flopping to the side over one ear and hanging there.

He fell backward onto Helen Ruth and the two of them disappeared between the chairs.

Hue stepped in front of Dulcie to block Clarke, his hands waving in front of him like he was going to cast a spell. At the last instant he flinched and stepped back, tripping over Dulcie's foot, sprawling off to the side.

Dulcie's eyes rolled back. She wavered for a second, then she dropped.

Her dress did not.

It disintegrated, spitting into the warm air like a burst feather pillow, each spinning pufflet pulsing its own unique color. The confetti of organza flakes fluttered in slow motion, then began to settle. Dulcie lay below the cloud on her side, her hair covering her face, her white silk slip speckled with scraps of wedding dress.

Clarke ran the last two steps to her, bent down, grabbed her under her arms, and began to drag her toward the house, away from the settling, rioting cloud of organza dust.

"Whiteley, put her down." Hue straightened himself upright, brushing dirt and cloth flakes off one arm.

Clarke put her down, breathing heavily, hoping they were far enough away now from the bulk of the cursed cloth. But Dulcie was still covered in the stuff. He began batting at her slip with both hands.

"Stop that," Hue said, holding up his fists like an amateur boxer and starting forward, ducking sideways to go around the settling cloud. "Just get away from her."

The cloud of cloth exploded, the concussion sending Clarke and Hue tumbling to the patio in opposite directions. A searing ball of green and purple flame roiled upward, spewing yellow-gray smoke as it rose.

On the other side of the smoke everyone screamed at once, chair legs scraping flagstone. From all around and underneath Dulcie, dozens of tiny balls of yellow-gray smoke puffed upward, leaving holes like cigarette burns in her slip. Something smelled like burning hair, and Clarke hoped it was the incinerated organza and not Dulcie.

Hue twisted himself into a sitting position, ran a hand through his hair, and looked at it with a sigh of relief. He turned. "Whiteley, what did you do?"

Through the thinning smoke, Clarke heard Helen Ruth scream, "Theobald, what did you do?"

Dulcie coughed and lifted her head slowly, raising herself up on her elbows. Her mouth fell open in a little O, her unfocused gaze following the column of smoke rising up from the spot where she had stood moments before. She blinked. "What did I do?"

"No," Clarke said. "This wasn't your fault. I never—"

The smoke began to swirl crazily, and Gory stepped through, waving his arms and coughing. "Well it's damn well somebody's fault." He shrugged out of his suit coat, snapped it open with a flourish, and wrapped it around Dulcie's shoulders. "And I aim to find out whose."

"Shall we—" Hue, an uncharacteristic look of utter bewilderment on his face, looked from Gory to Dulcie. "Shall we continue with the wedding?"

"You've got to be kidding," Dulcie said, waving a hand at the wreckage of her dress.

"Oh, I think it's too late for that, dear," Helen Ruth said. She reached down, plucked a bright red stole off the patio flagstones, and twirled it in the air.

Pastor Emmons was nowhere to be seen.

Helen Ruth strode calmly around the thinning column of colored smoke and stopped in front of Clarke, glaring straight into his eyes. "Clarke, I believe you have some explaining to do."

Helen Ruth had nerve, Clarke had to give her that. He did not know what Helen Ruth had done, or how she had done it, but he was damned well not going to take the fall for this.

5. A Profound Mismatch

To Clarke's surprise, Gory served the tea. Gory was now in the kitchen while the five of them—Clarke, Dulcie, Hue, Helen Ruth, and Bernard Theobald—sat in the dining room around the Hawthornes' immense oak table. Clarke had insisted, over Helen Ruth's objections, that Theobald join the discussion.

All of them were still in their wedding outfits. All except Darcie, who wore jeans and a Big Bopper T-shirt.

Gory returned from the kitchen wiping his hands together. He sat down at the head of the table—Dulcie and Hue on one side, Clarke and Theobald on the other, Helen Ruth at the far end—and leaned back and crossed his arms.

It felt like a scene from an Agatha Christie novel. Someone in the room was guilty, and all that was left was to trick the culprit into revealing their villainy.

"Clarke, why don't you start?" Gory said. "Explain how it's not your fault that your dress exploded and ruined my only daughter-in-law's wedding."

Hue sat forward, as if he were about to say something, then slumped back into his chair.

Clarke had no problem revealing his own part in the disaster. After all, he had gone ahead and made the dress, even knowing where the organza came from.

But he had no idea how to explain without accusing Gory's wife of sabotaging her own son's wedding. And without revealing that Dulcie had stolen Helen Ruth's wedding dress.

"Well—" Clarke said, with no idea what words would come next.

"It isn't Clarke's fault," Dulcie said. "I made him do it."

Clarke said, "That's not true, I—"

"Made him do what?" Gory asked.

"I made him put a maiden aura on the dress."

"A what?"

"Maiden aura. It glows pink to..." Dulcie looked down at her hands and folded them demurely. "To prove I'm a virgin."

Gory's cheeks bloomed a mottled pink.

Clarke stifled the urge to blurt out, "Yes, that's the color." Then he stifled the urge to laugh.

Gory glared the full length of the table at Helen Ruth. "I thought we were done with this nonsense."

Helen Ruth shrugged innocently.

Hue scratched the back of his head and looked puzzled. "What are we all talking about? Other than the exploding dress, I mean."

Gory said, "Thirty-three years ago your mother tried to impress me with a maiden aura at our own wedding. Failed miserably, didn't it, Bernie?"

Theobald, who had been analyzing his fingernails with profound interest, jerked upright from a slouch. He nodded slowly. "I took full responsibility for the failure." He licked his lips, then added, "I still do."

"A maiden aura," Clarke said, half to himself. Thirty-three years ago, the organza that Theobald used to make Dulcie's dress had been imbued with a maiden aura.

Helen Ruth lay a hand on Theobald's arm. "And I forgave

you long ago." She glared at Gory. "Even if my husband cares to hold a grudge."

Hue said, "What happened? Was it like what happened to Dulcie's dress?"

Helen Ruth said, "We don't need to rehash—"

"Yellow," Gory said. "I had not seen that particular disgusting shade of grayish, brownish yellow since my days on my grandfather's farm—"

Helen Ruth slammed her hand on the table. "Gorance Goldsmith Hawthorne, you will *not*."

Gory blushed again, appearing to swallow whatever barnyard image he had been about to conjure.

Yellow. That made no sense. A maiden aura that old, if it had any effect at all, would still glow pink. Assuming that Dulcie exhibited the appropriate characteristics.

And assuming there were no interference from, say, a weaver's wand.

Clarke turned and squinted suspiciously at Theobald, who sheepishly straightened his lapels with his thumbs.

Gory held up a placating hand. "The unnerving spectacle lasted only a second, Hue, and then was gone. But I assure you it was most disturbing. Most disturbing."

His eyes defocused, and for a moment the room was silent except for the ragged breathing all around the table. The room smelled like flop sweat. Clarke could not tell how much of the stink was his own.

Dulcie cleared her throat. "I have a confession."

All eyes turned toward her, all eyebrows raised.

She hesitated, then drew a deep breath. "I stole Helen Ruth's dress from the attic. I gave the organza to Clarke. He used that to make my dress."

Helen Ruth glowered. At Clarke. "You what?"

Clarke rolled his shoulders to buy time. "We needed fabric to replace the original dress after—"

"He didn't know," Dulcie said. "I told him I bought the fabric in Exeter."

Helen Ruth narrowed her eyes but said nothing.

"So that explains it, then," Gory said, nodding, lips pursed, as if he were trying to convince himself.

"Dad," Hue said, scratching the back of his head, "the dress exploded."

"Hmmm." Gory frowned.

Another long moment passed. The atmosphere felt humid, and not only from the ocean air.

Gory said, "Clarke, do maiden auras often explode?"

"No, sir. Even if the bride is not a— Even if conditions are not favorable, the worst that happens is that the magic fails. Unless—" This line of questioning could lead nowhere good, for him or for Dulcie. Clarke hesitated.

One word too late.

"Unless?" Gory said.

"I use a—" Clarke decided to switch pronouns. "We use a special kind of tears to make the magic. If they lack the requisite properties, that can cause a different kind aura. Results are unpredictable."

Clarke did not want to follow this line of reasoning, either. "The requisite property?"

"A virgin," Clarke said. "They must come from a virgin bride."

"The tears you used. Where did you get them?"

Dulcie said, "He got them from me, Mister Hawthorne."

Gory opened his mouth to say something, but Dulcie turned to face him full-on, her mouth in a tight little line.

Gory only spluttered, his cheeks once again turning mottled pink.

Clarke was starting to feel sorry for Gory. The man was only trying to find out what had gone wrong. Only trying to make things right for his family.

"But that doesn't..." Hue said, trailing off. "Dulcie is— You are— Aren't you... uh..."

"Shall we continue with the wedding?" Dulcie said, tilting her head and crossing her arms.

Hue appeared to swallow his tongue.

Clarke had to put an end to the conversation. And he knew how to do it.

At least, he thought he did.

All he had to do was 'fess up.

"I have a confession to make," he said, and steeled himself. "I never put the aura on the dress."

"Oh, no," Helen Ruth said.

"God!" Dulcie shouted, flinging her arms out to the sides. "What does a girl have to do to around here to prove she is a virgin?"

"No, that wasn't the reason. I believed you."

"Then why, Clarke?" Dulcie's voice wavered. Her lip trembled.

This was not going well.

"It was too risky to use your own tears. I chickened out."

"You promised!"

Gory leaned forward, one hand raised over the table. "But if there was nothing wrong with the dress..."

"Oh, there was something wrong with the dress." Clarke slowly pushed his chair back and rose to his feet, trying to appear dramatic. "And someone at this table can tell us what it was."

Clarke turned to Theobald. "What was on the weaver's wand that you gave to Helen Ruth?"

"Nothing," Theobald said, holding his hands up in surrender. "At least, nothing that would do *that*."

Gory said, "A weevil's what?"

"A weaver's wand. Theobald gave it to Helen Ruth just before the ceremony."

"I wondered what that thing was," Gory said. He looked at Helen Ruth, then back to Clarke. "Eh, what was that thing?"

"It gives the wielder power over the cloth that it made. That is the very shuttle that Theobald himself used to weave Helen Ruth's organza all those years ago, is my guess."

Theobald sputtered, "Yes, but—"

"You did this, Bernie?"

"Yes. No." Theobald looked confused. "It was just amplification. Helen Ruth said—"

Helen Ruth jumped to her feet, knocking her chair over. "You will *not* blame this on me, you charlatan."

Theobald shrank back in his chair. "I don't understand. Amplification wouldn't... unless..."

"I think you should leave, you two-bit huckster," Helen Ruth said. She pointed to the door. "Now. You've done enough damage to this family already." She reached toward Theobald.

"No!" Gory slammed his hand onto the table hard enough to rattle the chandelier overhead. "Nobody leaves this room until I understand exactly what is going on."

Clarke sat down.

Dulcie sat down.

Eventually, Helen Ruth sat down.

Gory let out a long, exasperated sigh and leaned back in his chair. "I'm feeling at sea here. Clarke, do you understand any of this?"

Helen Ruth said, "Obviously Bernard screwed up again. What more do you—"

Calmly Gory said, "Clarke?"

"Apparently, Bernie imbued the weaver's wand with some kind of amplification. And clearly it amplified something. Some magic that was already on the dress."

Gory's eyebrows rose. "Helen Ruth's maiden aura. The one that ruined our own wedding."

"It would seem that way," Clarke said. But it did not sound right. Even amplified, a maiden aura would not flare multiple colors, disintegrate into dust on the bride's body, and explode.

Unless.

Clarke looked at Dulcie.

No. He would not doubt her again. Even to himself.

He shrugged. "A catastrophic effect like that usually comes from a profound mismatch."

"Between me and the aura," Dulcie said, her voice icy. "Or between my tears and the aura."

Hue said, "What was the aura on the organza?"

"I told you dear," Helen Ruth said. "A maiden aura."

Hue shook his head. "But she's a maiden. And her tears are a maiden's tears. Clarke said—"

"Clarke is a charlatan just like Theobald." She placed her hands on the table as if to rise. "Really, Gorance, I think we've all had enough of this incompetent flimflammery for one day."

"I haven't," Dulcie said. She turned to Theobald. "What aura did you put on Helen Ruth's dress for her wedding? Think about what happened today. To my wedding dress. To what should have been the happiest moment of my life. Don't you think I deserve the truth?"

"I—" Theobald began.

Dulcie cut him off before he could answer. "What aura, really?"

Theobald sagged as if someone had let all the air out of him. Very softly he said, "Pregnancy."

"Oh, dear God," Clarke said. A virgin with a pregnancy aura. Amplified by a weaver's wand. "That explains it."

Gory said, "It most certainly does not. Bernard, why on earth would you put a pregnancy aura on a virg—" An insight flashed across his face. He frowned deeply and turned to his wife.

"It explains everything, dear," Helen Ruth said. "It explains why my wedding surprise for you went disgustingly wrong. Bernie put the wrong—"

"Not wrong," Theobald said, his trembling voice barely above a whisper.

"That makes no sense," Gory said. "My God, man, what are you saying?"

Theobald's face had gone pale, his eyes hollow. "I'm sorry, Dulcie. I did not know you were wearing the cloth from Helen Ruth's dress. I swear I did not know."

"So," Hue said, his face twisted grotesquely in unaccustomed thought. "Why didn't *your* dress explode, Mom?"

Dulcie said the words that were on Clarke's lips. "Because she was pregnant."

Theobald burst into chest-wracking sobs. "Forgive me, Helen Ruth," he said, his voice thin and pathetic. "I love you. I've always loved you. But I cannot perpetuate this lie any longer."

"What lie?" Hue said. "Somebody tell me what the hell is going on."

Gory tilted his head back and began to laugh, deep and verging on hysteria.

"Dad?"

Gory half composed himself and wiped the tears from under his eyes with his knuckles. He pointed at Theobald with a trembling finger. "There is your father, Hue."

Hue looked at Theobald, puzzled, and reached up to scratch the back of his head. His hand stopped in mid air and his eyes went blank. His fingers hovered above the slightly thinning hair.

Helen Ruth withered into a ball in her chair. In a small voice she said, "You should not have stolen my dress, Dulcie."

"So you blew it up while I was wearing it," Dulcie said wryly. "Yes, that seems fair."

Helen Ruth's cheeks puffed out, but she said nothing.

"Oh my God," Hue said, his gaze far away. "Fiona."

Theobald made a gurgling sound somewhere deep in his throat.

Dulcie said, "Who is Fiona?"

"Fiona Combover," Clarke said. "Somebody Hue dated once or twice a long, long time ago. Maybe we'll tell you all about it some other time. We'll all have a good laugh."

But before then, Clarke thought, we'll all have a good cry.

Author's Note

*Several years ago I invented a fun writing exercise for myself:
Write 60 opening lines in 60 minutes. That seemed like a fine
time limit. One opening line per minute. The idea was that,
stocked with a large pile of opening lines, I could start a story
any time I wanted. All I would have to do is copy an unused
line from the pile, paste it into a fresh manuscript file, and
start typing.*

*I didn't make it to sixty. In fact, I didn't make it to four.
I wrote three opening lines and quit.*

The first was:

> There are three things a taylor needs above all others:
> Needles, thread, and a fresh supply of tears.

*I had no idea of the story. I didn't even know what genre
the story would be. I didn't know the first thing about tailoring,
including how to spell it.*

*But the most intriguing thing I didn't know was: What the
heck did this opening line mean? Why on earth would a tailor
have such a great need of tears?*

*I revisited this languishing list of opening lines every
now and then for the next few years. But I didn't do anything with them.*

*Then one day I finished a story and didn't have any par-
ticular story to write next. So I opened my dinky list, grabbed*

the one about tailors, and started typing. I still had no idea where the story was going, or what the opening line meant, but I kept typing.

Then I got to the part where Gory calls Clarke incompetent. Clarke surprised me by announcing that he was indeed competent, but he was not magical.

Until that moment, I'd had no idea there would be magic in this story.

But now I knew. And suddenly I knew, more or less, what direction the story was headed.

I finished the story over the next few days. The original ending was quite different from the one you just read. My writing group hated it, and they were right. So I wrote a new ending.

I was especially delighted that Fiona Combover made an appearance at the very end. In the opening, I'd written a line about her as a kind of throwaway character, as a way to characterize Hue and his relationship with Clarke. Her reappearance made a lovely bookend for the story.

The remaining two opening lines are still trapped in that lonely file, arms crossed, scowling at me, waiting.

CARRION ROAD

Carla's feet hurt. Her heels twitched as she walked along the shoulder of Carrion Road. The back of her right shoe chafed against her heel. A blister seemed inevitable. Her purse smacked against her ribs and the strap bit into her neck. Ahead the shoulder of the road rolled off, and at the bottom of the small embankment a murky puddle refused to reflect the moonlight. Carla twisted off one shoe and then the other, tucked them under her arm, and stepped tenderly toward the embankment. The roadside gravel, which was cooler now that the sun had set, prickled the soles of her feet. She licked sweat off her lip.

"Fuck you, Eddie," she said to the quiet, still air. Not satisfied, she tried again. "Fuck you!" Better, better. "Fuck you, Edward Stewart Mann!" Yes, that was it.

She reached the edge of the puddle, hesitated. She leaned over and slid a finger along the raw place at the back of her foot. It stung at her touch, and her fingertip came away sticky. The blister had come and gone.

She could smell the puddle now, oily and vaguely biological. But her feet were sore enough and hot enough. She touched a toe to the water. It was warm, but cooler than the air, cooler than the gravel. She lowered her foot. The water was no more then two inches deep. The gravel at the bottom felt slick, and the water barely covered her toes. But it was cool. She lowered her other foot into the water and lingered, disgusted.

Carla hated weddings.

The embankment brightened, and Carla turned. A small car approached, its blue-white headlights blaring high beams. Carla raised her arm and squinted to block the glare, her shoes dangling from her hand.

Carla looked over her shoulder, calculating her options. A scrubby field spread off into the moonlight, separated from the ditch by a tangled wire fence. Somewhere beyond that, Carla presumed, was the Sacramento River or one of the dozens of channels that wound through the delta.

The car eased to the shoulder of the road and came to a stop. A Honda, small, like the one Eddie had rented. For a moment Carla thought Eddie had come back for her, but the rental had been dark blue. This one was silver or grey or white, Carla could not tell the exact color in the silver blue evening. She could not see through the windows. She unsnapped her purse and fumbled for her pepper spray.

The passenger window slid down to reveal a woman with long hair, dark and streaked with gray. The woman leaned toward Carla, biting her lip and squinting through rimless glasses. Beyond her a man wearing a light-colored chapeau angled his head to get a better look through the open window.

The woman said, "You tell us the story, we'll give you a ride. Deal?"

Carla laughed. She couldn't help it. "Does it have to be a good story?"

"No," the woman said, "but I bet it will be."

Carla started toward the car. "I haven't seen a car in thirty minutes. I appreciate your stopping."

"You haven't experienced Hank's driving yet." The woman twisted around in her seat, reached back, and opened the door. "I'm kidding about Hank's driving."

Carla tossed her shoes onto the floor and reached to brush the wet gravel from her feet.

"Don't worry about that," Hank said. "It's due for a vacuum anyway."

Carla slid onto the cloth seat. It was cool in the car. A newspaper lay folded on the seat. The car smelled the way Eddie's tiny rental car had, as if someone had smoked in it, but only months past. By the weak dome light she could see that Hank's chapeau was yellow, with a coarse weave that looked like burlap.

"Watch your dress when you close the door," the woman said. "Looks like you'll want to wear that one again if you can shake the memories. Real silk?"

"Seven hundred fifty dollars worth," Carla said, and wished she hadn't. The cost of her dress was a detail more personal than she ought to disclose to complete strangers on a deserted road in the middle of nowhere. She closed the door. The dome light went out, and the interior was lit only by the blue dashboard indicators and what little moonlight leaked in through the windows. She extended a hand between the front seats. "Carla."

"Vivian," the woman said, shaking Carla's hand. Vivian's hand was cool and slender, the skin sliding over small bones. "And Hank. Riordan. Hank and Vivian Riordan."

Hank shook Carla's hand and raised an eyebrow at her. "Carla?"

"Just Carla."

Hank nodded and released her hand.

"Cautious," Vivian said. "Prudent."

Hank shifted into drive and pulled the car out onto Carrion Road. As he drove, he rested his hand on the console between the front seats. Vivian laid her hand on his.

A happy, loving couple, Carla thought. Probably they were high school sweethearts and have been married for thirty-seven years. And they're on their way to visit their happy, loving daughter and their happy, loving grandchildren, who at age nine and eleven are well behaved and polite to strangers.

Hank said, "We're headed to Lodi. You?"

"Florida. Bradenton."

"That's a little out of our way." Hank winked and Vivian smiled.

Carla wanted to go home. Probably Sacramento didn't have flights this late. And she had no sense of how far Sacramento was from Carrion Road in the middle of nowhere. Or where Lodi was. What she wanted most was a bed. "Does Lodi have hotels?" Then she added, "Clean ones?" and regretted it.

Vivian laughed. "A blue silk dress hotel. Okay?"

"Perfect." A nice bed. A glass of wine. A good cry.

"We had a deal, dear," Vivian said, turning her head. "The story."

Carla bit her lip. She had agreed to this, but the story was none of Vivian and Hank's business. They were complete strangers. On the other hand, they were complete strangers. You could tell them anything, and at the end of the ride they would drive away and that would be the end of it. You could unburden yourself. And on a big fluffy bed in a blue silk dress hotel you could have a good laugh.

She could start at the end or the beginning or the middle. Or with the point. She said, "Fucking Eddie."

"Oh," said Vivian. "Fucking Eddie is never a good idea."

Carla laughed. "That was an adjective, not a verb."

"Well, adjectiving Eddie is not what I would call a healthy choice," Vivian said.

Hank shook his head. "No good can come of it."

"What?" Carla wasn't sure she had heard them right. Or maybe they hadn't heard her right.

Hank looked at her in the rearview mirror. "No good can come of adjectiving Eddie. It's not a healthy choice."

"I don't understand," Carla said.

"Well, it's your story, dear," Vivian said. "Is there more?"

Then Carla understood. They were playing with her head. Maybe this happy, loving couple amused themselves by picking up strangers and talking to them as if they were new to Planet Earth, just to see what would happen. Either that or they were crazy. Replaying the conversation in her head, she couldn't tell which.

Well if they were playing with her head, Carla could play along. If they were crazy, she would find out soon enough. Then she would have to figure out how to get out of the car. Back to walking Carrion Road in the dark. But in the meantime she could have a little fun. Improvise.

"Oh, there's more. I caught Eddie with the maid of honor. And the maid of honor turned out to be his cousin. And a man."

Hank frowned in the rearview mirror, then at Vivian. Vivian said, "What did you do?"

"What could I do? I stomped out of there in a royal huff. But I had nowhere to go. The lodge—the wedding reception was at a lodge in Carmel Valley—the lodge was full of Crevelings. That's the groom's family, and—"

Vivian said, "Nasty habit."

"What?" Carla started to replay her improvisation to see what habit she mentioned.

"Creveling. I've never understood why someone would do that."

"Why someone would…" Carla couldn't find the thread of meaning.

Hank said, "Crevel."

Vivian turned and regarded Carla with concern. "Are you okay, dear?"

Okay, this was not fun any more. If Hank and Vivian were playing with her head, it was working. And it was starting to seem cruel.

Carrion Road stretched out straight ahead beyond the reach of the headlights. Carla couldn't remember how long she and Eddie had been on the road, arguing, then arguing and insulting, then insulting and insulting, before Eddie pulled over and she got out and he drove away, straight ahead on Carrion Road until his car was gone in the distance. The road had been straight while they argued, straight while she walked and swore at the still air, straight while the Riordans listened to her story and turned her words into mysteries.

Eddie had decided without explanation to veer off I-580 somewhere east of Livermore. For a while they twisted through the delta, winding along rivers and channels, crossing over them, threading between them. They they began to argue. Just as Carla began to feel car sick, Eddie turned onto Carrion Road, and now two hours later here she was with two strangers that she was quickly taking a dislike to.

"Listen, I think I'd rather not talk about today. It's really unpleasant to talk about."

Hank slowed the car and flipped the turn signal.

"What are you doing?" But she knew. He was going to stop the car and kick her out.

"A ride for a story," Vivian said. "That was the deal."

These people were crazy. "Okay, look, this isn't funny."

"I wish it were funnier," Vivian said, turning and smiling at Carla. The smile was pleasant, without a hint of irony or malice.

The tires crunched in the gravel as the car rolled to a stop. The turn signal clicked like a metronome.

Hank reached a hand over his shoulder. "It was really nice meeting you, Carla."

"Thank you for your company, dear," Vivian said. "I hope we meet again."

"You're serious," Carla said.

Hank smiled. "This isn't funny."

Vivian said, "We miss you already."

They were still in the middle of nowhere. Carla had no idea how far it was to the next house. In fact, she couldn't recall seeing a house or a farm or a building of any kind anywhere on Carrion Road. Nor could she recall seeing a car other than the Riordans' going in either direction. She had not seen a streetlight since Eddie turned off I-580.

Carla imagined herself standing on the side of the road, no longer walking, only standing, her shoes dangling from her fingertips on of one hand and her purse dangling from the other. As creepy as Vivian and Hank were—and as cruel, if that's what they were—Carla did not want to be back on foot on Carrion Road.

"Listen, is your offer still open?"

"Of course," Vivian said.

Hank said, "We're not Indian givers."

"I'll tell you the story, then. And thank you again for giving me a ride."

Hank flipped the turn signal to the left, shifted into gear, and pulled back onto the road. The double yellow line extended as far as Carla could see. A double yellow line. No passing.

Vivian said, "You don't have to tell us to listen."

"What?"

"We're listening to you. You don't have to tell us to listen."

Another non sequitur, Carla thought, and mentally shrugged it off. She tried to think of a way to continue the soap opera story she was telling. She couldn't remember what she had said, or where she had left off. Maybe she could stall for time.

"What were the two of you doing out here in the middle of nowhere?"

Vivian shook her head. "When you give us a ride, we'll tell you the story."

That wasn't likely to happen. Carla would head east first thing in the morning. And she hoped never to come back to California, and certainly not to the Sacramento delta, which seemed to go on forever. "Are we still in the Sacramento delta?"

Hank shrugged. "Nobody can measure that." He flipped the directional signal and began to slow down.

So that's how it was. Carla had to keep telling the story. "I knew I shouldn't have come to this wedding." Maybe she could find a way to weave the Riordans' non sequiturs into the story, like improv.

"Everybody knew," Vivian said.

Everybody knew. Of course. Even the loving couple who would learn of Carla's and Eddie's and the Crevelings' existence only hours later knew. Everybody knew.

"But what they didn't know," Carla said, "what they couldn't know, was that the cake was poisoned."

Hank nodded. "And the poison had caked."

"And so it wasn't distributed evenly. And so only the bride's father ate the poison. So when Rhonda—that's the bride—when Rhonda danced with him for that first dance, he threw up all over the dance floor."

"The whole truth, so help me Rhonda," Vivian said.

"And as Rhonda tried to steady her father as he stumbled off the dance floor, he told her the while truth, the whole horrible truth about Benjie."

"You have to pay the piper," Vivian said.

Hank said, "Or the rats will never leave."

Carla tried to find a thread to follow. "And, and, rat poison, the rat poison in the cake, Benjie wanted all of the rat Crevelings to leave and take their nasty habits with them, so he put the rat poison in the cake, and that's the horrible thing that her father told her, and—"

Vivian's head snapped around and she glared at Carla. "You said nobody knew. Couldn't know."

"A deal is a deal," Hank said. The Honda's directional signal began ticking and the car slowed down.

The fucking car slowed down.

What the hell was wrong with these people? Carla snapped and screamed at Hank and Vivian and the car. "You can't stop. I did what you asked. You asked me for a story. I'm telling you a goddamned story. You can't stop. I have no idea where we are."

Vivian and Hank said nothing. The car crunched to a stop on the roadside gravel.

That was it. That was enough. Carla was done with Hank and Vivian Riordan. Done with their lunatic comments. Done with their cruel threats to stop the car every time the conversation violated their goddamned rules of conveyance.

She threw open the door and stepped one foot out onto the still warm gravel. The shoulder of the road rolled gently down to a ditch below. Wet footprints emerged from a murky puddle, and beyond the puddle a tangled wire fence stretched parallel to the road, and beyond the fence a scrubby field spread off into the moonlight.

Carla began to cry. She knew that if she stepped out of the car, she would be right back where she was thirty minutes ago, stranded in the moonlight by the side of the road in the middle of nowhere, screaming obscenities into the uncaring air. And she knew that there were no other cars on Carrion Road. Would never be another car on Carrion Road.

Her ankles started to throb.

"What do you want from me?"

In unison, Vivian and Hank said, "Tell us the story."

"Eddie wants me to marry him," Carla said. The Honda slowly accelerated onto Carrion Road, and Carla told the story. The wedding—Eddie's little sister getting married—had got him thinking about marriage again, and he was insisting. He brought it up a lot. Usually he would drop the subject and pout after a while.

But not today, driving in the rental car through this swamp toward Sacramento. Today he would not let go. "It's what people do when they love each other," he said, leaving the implication unspoken. The implication was what got Carla so angry. She did love him. It wasn't that she didn't want to marry him. She didn't want to be married at all, to anyone. They were happy enough the way they were. They loved each other. She woke up every day and she loved this man. Why couldn't he leave well enough alone?

"Is it the commitment? Is that the problem?" Of course that wasn't the problem. She was committed, to him, to the two of them as a couple, and yes, to her own happiness, dammit. She was happy with him. But once again Eddie couldn't let it go. Not today. He kept pushing. Don't you want this. Don't you care that. Don't you, don't you, don't you. Every question punctuated by a stab of his finger on the dashboard. Every question an insult.

And he turned onto Carrion Road.

Just leave it alone, dammit, Eddie. I love you, I do. What's wrong with what we have. Why must you always. Why must you. You never. You'll never be satisfied.

Do you want to be with me or not?

Of course I do. I'm with you right now.

Marry me, Carla. That's all I'm asking. What's so fucking wrong with that.

Why are you never satisfied? You're smothering me. Back off. Just please back the fuck off.

Right now, Carla. Yes or no? Right now.

Stop, Eddie. Please just stop.

He stopped the car. And then he drove away.

Vivian and Hank said nothing. Through the whole story, neither had uttered a word.

"That's all of it," Carla said. "What happens now?"

Hank continued driving. Carrion Road stretched straight ahead into the gloom.

Vivian said, "What happens now?"

"I mean, does this road go somewhere? Does it end?"

Hank said, "How does it end?"

It took Carla a moment to realize that they were asking about the story, what happens next, how it ends. "No, the story is over. Eddie drove away. Then you came. That's the end."

"Still telling it," Hank said, and waggled a finger to indicate the double yellow line passing by the car.

"Comedy or tragedy?" Vivian said.

Suddenly Carla knew the ending, and laughed. Comedy or tragedy? She would let Vivian decide that for herself. "And then I set Eddie free."

Hank put his hand on the console. Vivian laid her hand on his, and their fingers intertwined.

They drove on. Carrion Road curved gently to the right. In the distance a street light appeared, and beyond that an overpass.

AUTHOR'S NOTE

Carrion Road *began as an image: Carla walking along the side of a road, shoes dangling from her hands, yelling, "Fuck you, Eddie!" I knew Carla had dark hair. I knew the road was on the outskirts of a city. I knew Eddie had abandoned her by the side of the road. I did not know why. I did not know what would happen next.*

Once upon a time I had the idea that before I could write a story, I had to know the story. So I waited for a story.

The story never came.

And the image haunted me.

Then one day I wanted to write. I had no particular story in mind, but I remembered this haunting image.

I began typing.

Almost immediately, I was surprised to learn that the road was nowhere near a city. It was in the middle of the Sacramento Delta, a very long road with no houses or buildings for miles around.

I was intrigued when the car stopped. I didn't know who was in the car. I was as wary as Carla was.

So I kept on typing.

Vivian and Hank amused me, and that drew me forward, into the story. Carla was tired and angry and frustrated and a little scared. But Vivian and Hank were odd and curious. They amused me.

They did not amuse Carla.

And that amused me.

So I kept on typing.

I stayed on that long lonely road with Carla, as puzzled as she was. No other cars came by. The road went on and on, without the slightest curve.

After a while, Vivian and Hank started to scare me, too.

So I kept on typing, hoping Carla would find a way to get us safely home.

REFUND

1. WYDIYCA

G EOFF WHEEZED as he reached the third floor of the training center. The elevator would have been faster, but he wanted extra time to prepare for his confrontation with Anderton. No, that was a lie. The truth was that he wanted to stall. So he had hauled his overweight, under-exercised body up the three flights of stairs.

And now he needed to catch his breath. That would take a good two minutes. He put out a hand, leaned against the wall, and waited for his heart to slow down.

Anderton stepped out the classroom door into the hallway. "Ah, Mister Palmenter! I thought I heard a noise out here. I am delighted that you arrived early. You can help me set up." He spun back into the classroom. Anderton's whistling echoed down the hall, some old tune by Neil Diamond or Barry Manilow.

This wasn't going to be easy, Geoff knew. Anderton was a Certified Master Negotiator, a fact that he mentioned at least twice in every class.

When Geoff reached the classroom, Anderton stood in front of the table at the front of the room, tacking a poster to the wall with blue putty. "WYDIYCA: What'll You Do If You Cannot Agree?" That had been the first lesson in the first class. If you know your WYDIYCA, you will always know when it's time to walk away from the negotiation.

Geoff noticed the informal contraction in the slogan. It was, he now knew, at odds with the way Anderton spoke. He never used contractions, even when he read the slogan. "What will you do," he said. Geoff and Lyndie had playfully mocked Anderton's almost comically formal tone. But Geoff hadn't noticed the contraction when he first saw the poster, five weeks ago.

Five weeks ago. Tuesday, the third of June. That was the day Geoff met Lyndie. Lyndie would be arriving by seven o'clock, in time for the final class. Geoff needed to be done by then. Done and gone. He couldn't bear to see her again. Not now, so soon after—

He shook off the thought and looked at his watch. Twenty minutes. "Mister Anderton, we need to talk."

"Can we talk while you put Yoda up on the wall?" Anderton pointed toward the table. Several posters lay curled into tubes. One was held flat with rolls of blue masking tape and packets of blue putty. Yoda glared up from behind a blazing blue lightsaber. Above Yoda, glowing yellow block letters read, "USE THE FORCE!" Below was the caption, "Don't be afraid to use your power!"

Geoff had not seen the Yoda poster before. This must be today's lesson. Another contraction. Surely Anderton would say, "Do not be afraid." Geoff wouldn't be around to hear it, but he could apply the lesson anyway, right now. He would use his power. If Anderton refused to refund Geoff's money, Geoff would sue him. How was that for a WYDIYCA?

Geoff straightened. "No, sir, I want your full attention for this."

"I see." Anderton motioned to one chair and sat in another. "What is on your mind?"

Geoff remained standing. "I want a refund."

Anderton frowned and nodded. "You are dissatisfied?"

Here we go, Geoff thought. "No, I'm not."

"Can you tell me why?"

"I don't have to tell you." Geoff pulled a folded sheet of paper from his shirt pocket, the class description he had printed from Anderton's website. He unfolded it and pointed to the guarantee written in bold letters across the bottom.

"That is correct. You need not tell me," Anderton said, not bothering to look at the printout. "But you seemed to be enjoying the class, and doing well, so I am curious."

"I'd rather not say." Rather not say that he was too heartbroken to be in the same room with Lyndie. Rather not say that without the refund he couldn't afford to sign up for the next offering of the class. Rather not say that if he wasn't certified by the end of the summer, his boss would bust him from sales down to a desk job. Rather not tell his opponent— check that: his "negotiating partner"—just how little negotiating power he had.

Anderton said, "What was the first moment that you spent on the class?"

The first moment? Anderton was playing some kind of game here, and Geoff didn't have time for games. "I don't want to negotiate this. I just want the refund. The website says satisfaction guaranteed, no questions asked."

"Actually, it says no such thing. I do need to ask a question or two. I need the information to figure out how to refund you."

"What's to figure out? Write me a check. Seven hundred dollars."

Anderton laughed. "A check? Oh, my dear boy, you seem to have misunderstood the guarantee."

Geoff waved the class description again. "It says right here that if I'm not completely satisfied, you'll give my money back."

Anderton shook his head. "Read it again."

Geoff read the guarantee aloud. "If you are not completely satisfied that the class was worth every minute of your time, we will cheerfully give you a full refund."

"You see?"

"See what? It says 'full refund.'"

"It says not one word about money."

Geoff shook his head. Anderton was trying to trick him somehow. "Road apples, sir. What the hell else are you going to refund? My wasted time?"

Anderton smiled. "Exactly."

"Look, enough with the head games. Just give me the damned refund."

"That is exactly what I intend to do, Mister Palmenter." Anderton stood and touched his fingertips together lightly. "Humor me with just this one question. What was the first moment that you spent on the class?"

"You mean the first day of class?"

"If that is when you think the class began for you, then yes. For some people the first moment is earlier."

Geoff didn't like this. He was running out of time before the other students showed up. Before Lyndie showed up.

He thought for a moment. "I guess it started with my boss's email, the Thursday before the first class. He said I had to—"

Anderton rotated his hands so that his thumbs and index fingers formed a circle and his pinkies pointed at Geoff.

"—take this class or give up my—"

Geoff stopped. He felt dizzy and his stomach writhed. He needed to sit down.

But he was already sitting down. Anderton was gone. The classroom was gone. Geoff was in his cubicle on the third floor of Formby's Family Foundry, sitting in his rickety five-wheeled chair, gripping the edge of his desk with one hand.

He leaned over and threw up into his wastebasket.

Geoff's computer chirped. A new email message had arrived in his inbox.

2. Pay Attention

THE NEXT TIME Geoff entered the classroom was either five days later or five weeks earlier, depending on how one reckoned these things. The third of June again. Anderton stood near a corner in the front of the room, his back to the door, holding the WYDIYCA poster against the wall with one hand, pressing a small ball of blue putty onto the wall with the thumb of his other hand.

Anderton stopped rolling the putty and tilted his head. "I am trying to decide, Mister Palmenter, whether I am surprised that you have returned." He turned and smiled at Geoff, rubbing his thumb with his fingers. "I am leaning toward not surprised."

That answered Geoff's first question. Anderton remembered him. This wasn't going to be easy. Naturally.

Anderton's grin widened. "What can I do for you this time?"

"I want to sign up for your class," Geoff said. He tried to chuckle nonchalantly, but it came out as a grunt. "Again."

Anderton picked up a small cloth from the table, rubbed his fingers on it, and gave a slow, exaggerated stage frown, the kind meant to play to the back row of a theater. "And here I was under the impression that you were dissatisfied with my instruction."

"Oh, no," Geoff said. "Your teaching was fine."

"The content, then?"

"Hey, you said no questions asked."

Anderton's grin returned. An exaggerated stage grin. "That was for your refund, which I have already paid in full. How can I be sure you will not seek a second refund five weeks hence?"

"No refunds this time. I promise." Geoff held up three fingers of each hand. "I'll put it in writing if you like."

"Ah, in writing." Anderton nodded, and his smile seemed more genuine. "Let that be the first of our conditions."

"The first?"

"What makes you so eager to attend this class a second time?"

"Well, technically, it will be the first time—"

"Road apples, Mister Palmenter." Anderton smiled wryly. "You want something from me. Please do me the courtesy of respecting my time and my good humor, which I assure you is limited."

"I apologize, Mister Anderton. Look, I need this certificate. I need it, okay?"

"Did you not need it when you first attended?"

"Well, yes, but that was different."

"In what way?"

"Well, I... uh..."

Anderton gestured toward the table three rows back, where Geoff and Lyndie had sat throughout the class. "Something about your negotiating partner, perhaps?"

Geoff's gut suddenly felt hollow. Apparently Anderton was observant. Of course he was observant. The lesson of week four had been PAY ATTENTION! And it wasn't as if Geoff and Lyndie had been subtle in their affections.

Maybe Geoff should just come clean. It wasn't as if his reason for bailing out of the earlier class was shameful. Embarrassing, sure, but nobody ever died of embarrassment. Maybe a little vulnerability would even help this negotiation.

And maybe Anderton knew the whole story anyway. If he could send people back in time, who knew what else he could do? For all Geoff knew, Anderton was omnipotent.

"Listen, Lyndie was the reason I cancelled before." Geoff paused. Vulnerability was hard. "No, actually, the reason is that I am a coward. Was a coward. She and I had just had a fight, and I couldn't face her for the last class. So I bailed out."

"I see," Anderton said. "You do realize, of course, that Miss Littleton is again—still—registered for this workshop. I recall that she was the first to arrive for the first session, quite early." Anderton looked at his watch.

Geoff did realize that. He'd had five days since he went back in time to think about her. And to try not to think about her. And to try not to feel the sucking vortex of hope and embarrassment and trepidation and despair that he felt every time he thought of her. Every time he tried not to think of her. Of course he realized she'd be here.

Geoff nodded. "She's one reason I want to take the class again."

Anderton smiled in what seemed like genuine amusement. "Oh, my dear young man. You have no idea of the challenge you have set for yourself."

"But do you…" Geoff wasn't sure he wanted to finish the question. Wasn't sure he wanted the answer. "Do you know—"

Anderton grinned. "You want a second bite at that lovely unsuspecting young woman's apple."

"Well, that's a crude way to—"

Anderton waved a hand to dismiss Geoff's objection. "And you say you need the certificate?"

In for a penny, in for a pound. Or seven hundred dollars. "Or my boss will fire me."

"I am willing…" Anderton paused, his open hands forward in a gesture of magnanimity. "To accept your registration for the sum of fourteen hundred dollars, non-refundable."

"Fourteen hundred? But your website says seven hundred."

"Seven hundred dollars per workshop."

"But you already gave me the refund."

Anderton nodded. "Which you are free to keep, if you have no further need of my instruction."

Geoff reached for his checkbook.

3. PREPARATION

LYNDIE NEVER SHOWED UP for that first class. And Geoff was absent, too, in his own way—physically present but mentally elsewhere, mentally everywhere, trying to find Lyndie, or at least clues to where she might be.

He sat in the same seat at the same table, smack in the middle of the classroom, that he had sat in before, for each of the five classes he had attended. Beside him, empty, was the seat where Lyndie should be, where Lyndie had always been, where she had been when they met.

"Mister Palmenter?" Anderton's voice.

Geoff blinked. Anderton smiled at him, eyebrows arched. Twenty students looked at him, some snickering. Apparently Anderton had asked a question that Geoff was expected to answer.

"What?" Geoff said.

Snickering turned to guffaws.

"You seem distracted," Anderton said, and turned to another student, the one who sat in front of Lyndie. Where Lyndie should be. "Mister Holbein?"

"Preparation," Holbein said. Anderton nodded, satisfied, then winked at Geoff and grinned. Geoff could not guess what the question might have been. He would have to pay more attention, if he could get his mind off Lyndie.

But he could not.

Anderton invited the students to pair up for the class's first exercise, a series of interactions about being prepared or unprepared for a negotiation. Geoff vaguely noted that he had somehow paired up with Holbein. Instead of Lyndie. Who wasn't there.

Geoff remembered everything about the first time he had done this exercise—Lyndie's smile as she shook his hand, the crooked front tooth. The gentle, sweet fragrance as she shook his hand. The slight southern lilt as she introduced herself. The way time sped up and slowed down at the same time.

He remembered every word they said as they role-played awkwardly at negotiating, first without a WYDIYCA and then with. First she played the boss and he negotiated for a raise. Then he played a car salesman and she negotiated for a lower price. And beneath the facade of their roles, they negotiated something more.

"Fascinating," Holbein said. "You know, you're very good at this."

"What?" Geoff said.

"Don't be so modest," Holbein said, laughing. He pointed a thumb at Anderton. "You could teach this class instead of Mister Stuffy."

"Tell my boss."

Holbein took a long breath. "Hey, do you think you might want to maybe go for coffee afterward?"

"Okay," Anderton said in a loud voice, and clapped his hands to break up the exercise. "Let us talk about how that went. What surprised you about your negotiations?"

Geoff was even more absent for the last half of the class. He thought about the five days since Anderton had flung him back in time, about how he had tried not to think about Lyndie, about how he had tried to find her. He walked by her apartment building three times, and the only light in the window was the one on the automatic timer. He waited twice outside McLin and Gagnon, the law office where Lyndie interned as a legal assistant, as her colleagues filed out after work. He spent three long evenings at Corbin's, her favorite after-work coffee shop. He brunched on Sunday at Chez Ami, her favorite weekend brunch spot. He thought about calling her, but could not think of a pretext. He entered her phone number by heart into his contacts, only to remove it, only to enter it again. He thought about driving the 800 miles south to Goldsboro, North Carolina, where Lyndie's mother would, within the next four weeks, suffer the stroke that would end her life and trigger the argument that would end Geoff and Lyndie's romance. But even if Lyndie was in Goldsboro, Geoff could think of no plausible way to explain his presence there, or to arrange an "accidental" meeting.

Geoff had considered the possibility that he had not looped back to his own past at all, but into an alternate timeline where Lyndie did not exist. He brushed the thought out of his mind more than once. Maybe there were rules to time loops that prevented him from meeting Lyndie before the appointed time. Geoff caught himself weighing which scenario was more plausible, and laughed. How did any of this make sense? And who said the universe had to make sense?

So Geoff had abandoned trying to figure out what was happening, what had happened, what would happen, and thought about Lyndie, and tried not to think about Lyndie, and waited until the appointed time, when he would meet her in the class and negotiate a raise and touch her hand and breathe her air and fall gently into her southern accent.

Now the appointed time had come and gone, and Lyndie's chair remained empty, and Geoff was lost in time.

4. Brown Bag

For the next week Geoff relied on routines to guide him through the day. His boss invited him to give a "brown bag lunch talk" about the WYDIYCA technique, and he sleepwalked through that without embarrassing himself. Geoff was wryly amused to learn that most of his colleagues had never heard of the idea. And yet they had somehow been successful for years, and he was ordered to take remedial training or "seek alternate employment opportunities." Twice Geoff had started to explain The Road Apples Retort, but caught himself just in time. Road Apples was the topic of week five, still nearly four weeks into the future. And Anderton was notoriously close to the vest about the topics of future classes. "If you really need to know, you will have to be sure to attend next week," he would say. Two of Geoff's colleagues had attended the workshop—voluntarily, not on the boss's orders—and he would not want to invite unanswerable questions about how he could know what he could not yet know. How do you tell your colleagues that you've been sent back in time?

5. Beemans and Clove

Geoff slowly climbed the training center stairs for the second week's class. At the top of the stairs, he unwrapped the last stick of clove gum from Lyndie's packet and popped it into his mouth. He winced. He was coming to hate the taste and the waxy texture. But the flavor and smell brought intense memories of Lyndie.

Twelve days earlier (or four weeks later), Geoff had abandoned the negotiation workshop because he couldn't bear to see Lyndie. Now he considered abandoning it again, because he couldn't bear not to see her.

He stepped through the classroom door, and there was Lyndie in her usual chair, biting her pen, flipping through the spiral-bound booklets of workshop handouts, blue for week one and yellow for week two. He half expected her to look up and smile at him—and he half expected to turn and run—but she did not.

Anderton stood hunched over the table at the front of the room, licking the tip of his index finger and flipping through his lecture notes. He looked up and smiled at Geoff, then nodded in Lyndie's direction, a cautionary expression on his face.

Geoff walked around the back of the room, then forward to his seat. His breathing was ragged and his gum had gone stale. He pulled out his chair, which scraped along the floor.

Lyndie continued studying the handouts. Probably trying to catch up after missing the first class.

Geoff sat down, and his chair scraped again. This time Lyndie looked at him, still biting her pen. She frowned slightly. Had Geoff annoyed her with his scraping?

He wanted to leap up, take her in his arms and whisper I'm sorry, I love you, I let you down, I love you, please forgive me. Instead he smiled weakly, and croaked, "Hi. Are you new?"

Her brow furrowed.

Was that some sort of cross-time recognition? Or was she just trying to figure out how to respond to his ridiculous question?

For the first time, she spoke. "Is that clove gum I smell?" Her nose wrinkled.

Geoff gagged. On their third date (five weeks ago or two weeks from now) they had each bought a packet of gum at the Kittery Trading Post—clove for her, Beemans for him. They had laughed about how they loved this stuff as kids, and didn't even know it was still for sale. They each simultaneously popped a stick into their mouths, grimaced, and laughed again. The flavor lasted for about three minutes, then the gum became waxy and flat and a little sour. For the next hour, they debated. Had the gum changed in fifteen years, or had they? Finally Lyndie said with conviction, "This is exactly the flavor I remember," and Geoff concurred. Then she handed him her packet of clove gum, and he put it in his pocket with his Beemans.

Now, sitting for the first time in the place where Geoff had met her, Lyndie looked mildly disgusted.

Geoff felt dizzy. She was supposed to be smiling at him by now. He was supposed to be laughing at their roleplaying from the week before. He was supposed to be working up the nerve to ask her on a date. But here she was frowning, almost recoiling from him. Had Geoff confounded the space-time continuum by chewing a stick of gum two weeks before he bought it? Could the universe really be so fragile, or so cruel?

Geoff looked at Anderton, who watched him and Lyndie with a blank expression. What the hell had Anderton done to him? Geoff had only wanted a refund, only wanted to get away, only wanted to get his head straight. Only wanted to wallow for a while alone in his misery, without the pressure of his teetering job and the class and the impending certification test to worry about. He had only wanted a little time.

6. How Fascinating

THE LESSON OF THE SECOND CLASS was about the How Fascinating technique, a way of regaining your balance when you are surprised in a negotiation. When Anderton announced the roleplaying exercise, Geoff looked at Lyndie, and she looked at him. She opened her mouth to say something.

Holbein piped in. "Hey, buddy. Are you ready to show me how it's done again?"

Geoff couldn't very well tell Holbein to buzz off, could he? Couldn't very well say Holbein, old chum, it's been swell working with you. But if it's all the same with you I'd rather fall in love with Lyndie, here. Look into her eyes and tell me you would do otherwise. And I know it's going to happen, because it already happened. In the future.

A middle-aged woman (whose name Geoff thought might be Shelby) tapped Lyndie on the shoulder. Shelby had been the odd person out in the first class, and had joined two other people to make a practice team of three. Without looking back at Geoff, Lyndie got up and took the seat next to Shelby.

So Geoff negotiated with Holbein, and Holbein with Geoff, and Geoff could think only about southern accents and the Kittery Trading Post and the folly of telling the woman who is falling in love with you that you can't accompany her to her mother's funeral because you need this class, you need this certificate, you need this job, and you're so, so sorry.

By the time the How Fascinating exercise ended and Lyndie returned to her seat next to him, Geoff ached with frustration. He wanted to pick up his relationship with Lyndie where it had left off, but of course he could not do that.

So he would have to start over. But even starting over was not possible. He had changed, and not for the better. Before, he had been optimistic and confident and uncharacteristically charming. Now he felt lost and desperate. Why on earth would Lyndie find that attractive?

But he had to try.

7. ROAD APPLES

WHEN ANDERTON DISMISSED THE CLASS, Geoff packed up his class materials as he tried to think of something worthy to say to Lyndie. But as he gathered up his notes and his yellow class handouts, he saw that Lyndie was already halfway to the door. He jumped up and ran after her.

He caught up to her at the top of the stairs. "Lyndie, wait," he said, sounding more breathless than he wanted. What could he say next that wouldn't sound like some jerk hitting on her out of the blue, based on knowing nothing of her but the way she looked? But of course he was hitting on her. And of course it would sound like it was out of the blue. And of course he couldn't tell her that he knew so much more of her. She had already been put off by his first lame words to her. What would she think of, "Hi, I'm from the future, where you and I were briefly in love?"

So he said, "It was nice to meet you," and stuck out his hand.

To Geoff's surprise, Lyndie smiled and laughed, and shook his hand. "Charmed, I'm sure," she said. Then her smile faded, and she looked away.

Geoff said, "Hey, do you want to drop by Corbin's for some coffee?" Like a jerk.

She looked at him for a long moment. "Do you know—" She stopped.

Of course he didn't know Corbin's. Not in Lyndie's time-line. Lyndie had introduced him to the place.

"I haven't been, myself. But some of the guys at work were raving about it," Geoff said. His mouth was dry.

"Your friends have good taste," Lyndie said, and smiled weakly. "But, listen, I'm a little under the weather right now."

"Some other time, then?" Geoff said. Exactly like some jerk.

"I don't know." Lyndie reached out and put a hand on Geoff's arm, then drew it away.

"I'm sorry. I don't mean to—"

"Oh, no, you seem very nice," Lyndie said. "The thing is, my mother is in the hospital, and I'm just not in the mood for company."

The hospital? This was all wrong. This was not how things were supposed to go—had gone. Lyndie's mother's stroke was not supposed to happen for nearly another two and a half weeks, until three days before the fifth class. This was all wrong.

"Listen," he said, "I think I'll just go. I'm not usually so forward. I've never hit on anybody like this before."

"Road apples!" she sang, drawing out each syllable, the first word higher pitched, the second lower. In exactly the comical way Anderton had taught them two weeks ago, three weeks in the future.

Lyndie clapped her hand over her mouth.

Of course it was road apples. Geoff had been exactly that forward before. Exactly one time. With Lyndie.

And she knew.

Mimicking Anderton's deliberate cadence, Geoff said, "But you must never, ever, sing it out loud." He tapped the side of his head. "Only in here."

Lyndie's eyes grew wide and her hand fell from her mouth. "Oh my God, Geoff."

Geoff reached into his pocket. "I'm out of clove gum, but would you like a stick of Beemans?"

8. LEAN FORWARD

A T THE FAMILY GATHERING after Lyndie's mother's funeral, Geoff felt like an intruder. In this timeline he had not yet met Aunt Ruthie, Uncle Mason, the "dozen cousins," or Nana Fogg. They all regarded him suspiciously, and spoke to him in clipped sentences if at all.

But Lyndie had introduced him as her boyfriend, and that had more than made up for any awkwardness he felt.

Afterward, they drove north on the interstate listening to the windshield wipers thwack out a beat in the rain. Lyndie was mostly quiet in the passenger seat. Eventually she reached over and squeezed his hand. "I'm really grateful that you came with me, Geoff. You don't know how much it meant to me. Means to me."

Geoff squeezed gently in return. "I think I do."

"I hope taking time off work doesn't get you into trouble."

"Well if it does, that's okay with me," Geoff said. And he meant it.

A moment later Lyndie laughed. "And I'm sorry we had to miss the third class. The 'Lean Forward' technique was my favorite."

Geoff remembered, and smiled. "That roleplay was when I knew I loved you."

"That's two of the first three classes I've missed in this timeline," Lyndie said. "Do you think Anderton will let me make it up?"

Geoff grinned and shook his head. "Well, if not, you can always ask for a refund."

Author's Note

Some time in 2008, the central idea of this story came to me all at once: When our hero demands a refund, he receives his refund not in money, but in time. Then he realizes that he has an opportunity to repair a horrible mistake he made with his girlfriend.

I wrote the first scene quickly, and submitted it as part of my writing group's annual "blind submission" meeting. As I recall (vaguely—it was a long time ago), they liked the scene.

Then I set the story aside for a few years. I don't know why.

When I finally resumed the story, I knew I wanted a happy ending, but didn't know how I would get there.

So I started typing.

I especially enjoyed inventing fanciful-but-plausible names for negotiation techniques. (Invention of the actual negotiation techniques is left as an exercise for the reader.)

Two of Anderton's techniques are real techniques translated into fictional form. The WYDIYCA technique (what'll you do if you can't agree) is a rewording of the famous BATNA technique (best alternative to a negotiated agreement) from Fisher and Ury's groundbreaking book Getting to Yes.

The How Fascinating technique actually goes by that name, though it is not a negotiation technique. It is a technique for learning. I learned it from Evan Gardner and Willem Larsen's marvelous language-learning class called Where Are Your Keys. During the practice sessions, whenever you make a mistake, you (and everyone else in earshot) waggle your hands in the air and shout, "how faaaaascinating!" This silly technique is remarkably effective at turning what might otherwise feel stressful into a whole bunch of fun.

Of course, there is no reason you couldn't use the How Fascinating technique in negotiations, though maybe it would best to shout only in your own head.

Finally, please note that I am a much bigger fan of Beemans and Clove gum than are Geoff and Lyndie.

FUNHOUSE

Kippy was screaming no more than ten feet away, but the dim funhouse lights had gone out, and me and Davy couldn't see him in the dark. Davy jerked backward right in front of me and I bumped into him and he giggled. The air inside the funhouse was as hot as the Sacramento summer, and damp and sour and disgusting. It smelled like the locker room in the gym at school, like old sweat socks dipped in old puke.

Something tickled my neck and I jumped and screamed and Davy shrieked with laughter. I slapped at the thing on my neck. Just a piece of string dangling off the dark cloth strips that hung from the ceiling.

Kippy screamed again. "Mark! Davy! It's got me, you guys! Love of Jesus you guys, help me!" I'd never heard Kippy scream like that, like he was going to wet himself. I didn't know if he was hamming it up to scare us, or if he was really screaming like a girl or what.

Davy whispered, "Flashlight. Watch your eyes."

Then his little flashlight flickered on and in the yellow light we saw the thing that had Kippy. It was a big zombie, adult size, bigger than Kippy. Kippy's eyes were wide open and his mouth was wide open. The zombie had Kippy's head in its hands and it looked like it was going to take a big bite. Then it turned to us and it only had one eye. The other eye was dangling out of its socket on some stringy thing, and it wobbled back and forth on its cheek. Its face was dripping like silly putty. It was like the best zombie makeup I'd ever seen. It looked like you could see its teeth and its wriggling tongue right through a hole in its cheek.

"Freaking awesome," I said.

Davy pointed and howled in laughter.

"Run," Kippy said.

The thing poked its elbows out to the sides and you could see its muscles bunching up through the holes in its raggedy red flannel shirt, and the back of Kippy's head popped off and stuff spilled out and the thing stuck its face in it.

Jesus god it was some mad killer dressed up like a zombie.

Davy jumped up and the back of his head mashed me in the face and I fell over backward and he landed on me. The flashlight rolled under some dangling cloth and went out. I reached for it but the floor was sticky and Davy rolled off me and said, "Leave it. Go. Back the way we came."

He was my little brother and I should have been telling him what to do and not the other way around, but I wasn't going to argue. Part of me thought it wasn't right to leave Davy's best friend there with that monster doing what it was doing to his head. But every other part of me knew it was too late for Kippy.

"Run! Now!" Davy may have been two years younger than me, but he was always smarter since the day he was born.

I rolled onto my hands and knees and crawled back toward the mirrors, and Davy was right behind me, shoving his shoulder against my butt, whispering, "Go, go!"

My teeth caught on something and it hurt like heck, a gash in my lower lip from where Davy had mashed me with his head. I could taste the blood and it felt like there was a lot of it. I felt wobbly and I wanted to spit but I didn't want to crawl in my own blood.

Behind us the zombie was making spongy bubbling noises and I was almost glad I couldn't see.

My face smacked into the leather door that separated Undead Alley from the Hall of Mirrors. I batted it aside with a sweep of my arm and crawled through. The lights were out in the Hall of Mirrors, too, but the light from a blue exit sign—or maybe it was several signs—bounced and reversed among the mirrors. I could see my face in four directions, illuminated by a faint, ghostly glow.

Kippy had stopped screaming. I resisted the urge to turn around to see what was happening to him. I swallowed a mouthful of blood and nearly gagged.

"Move!" Davy said, and shoved me forward with his hand. He crawled through and the leather door flapped closed. "Get up."

I stood up and started to move toward the exit sign.

"Not that way. Follow me." He ducked sideways, between two mirrors.

I grabbed him. "Davy, that's not the right way. We came in from back there." I pointed behind me.

He wriggled and shook me off. "Exit signs," he said, and kept moving. "I saw it on the side of the building before we came in."

"Davy, no, that sign is backwards. It's a mirror."

He turned right and disappeared and split into two. Half of him went to the right and half to the left. He seemed to be looking both ways at once, like that Roman god that looked into the past and the future.

I stepped in the direction he had gone, and was lost. "Davy, which way did you go?"

A hand grabbed my shoulder and spun me around and I screamed.

But it was only Davy, holding a finger up to his lips. He pointed over his head. It was the real exit sign. Below that was a door with a bar running from side to side. He pushed on the bar and the door swung open, and the full glare of the afternoon sun hit us square in the face.

"Oh, no," Davy said, his voice wavering.

It took my eyes a moment to adjust. Beyond Davy, William Land Park spread off in the distance, the grass still miraculously green in the late summer heat. I should have seen families and couples and business groups grilling burgers and flying Frisbees and tossing balls to dogs. But it looked like half of the people had decided instead to take naps in the sun, all at once. And the other half had decided to chase each other in a weird, lurching game of tag.

But then I saw that some of the nappers were in pieces, and all of them were covered in blood. And the people playing tag were hitting each other with sticks and poking each other with shish kebab skewers and scratching at each other's faces. And everyone who was not napping or lurching was screaming.

"Zombies," Davy said.

I looked down. The funhouse was on a slope at the edge of the park, and the floor was four feet above the grass on this side. "How are we going to get past them?"

"We jump, then run like heck around the edge of the funhouse before they see us. If the coast is clear, we run into the zoo. They'll have shotguns there."

I had no idea if they had shotguns in the zoo, but Davy seemed sure. I nodded, though he was still looking out over the horrible scene, holding the door open with his hand. He crouched to jump.

A greenish-grey hand reached under the door and yanked it, hard. The door slammed against the side of the funhouse and Davy stumbled. I grabbed at his dark blue T-shirt, caught it by the neck hole as he fell, and yanked upward. I heard the shirt tear, and felt it, but Davy flopped past me and thudded onto the floor behind me.

In the full daylight I could see that the thing looking stupidly up at me was no person dressed in a zombie costume. There was a hole in the side of its head, and there was nothing inside the hole that I could see, and flies buzzed in and out. One ear had flopped onto the side of its neck, stuck there by a smear of purple black goo.

One of its eyes blinked at me, then the other. It made a *tsuk tsuk* sound like it was trying to smack its lips, but it didn't have any lips, and its tongue flipped wildly behind its few remaining teeth. The muscles of its mangled cheeks bunched, and I thought maybe it was trying to smile. It stepped forward and reached toward me, but there was no hand on that arm, just a gristly stump. It stopped and frowned and looked at where its hand should have been. It smelled like the transfer station on a hot day.

I gripped the sides of the door frame and lifted one sneakered foot.

"Don't touch it!" Davy shouted.

I kicked out anyway, and caught the zombie right in the forehead with the cushioned heel of my sneaker. Its head snapped back, then forward, and it fell over backward, reaching out with its missing hand to break its fall. I heard a sickening snap, and the thing made a keening, gurgling, farting sound, and I realized the sound was leaking out from underneath a flap of skin covering a hole in its chest.

The putrid thing twisted and began to sit up.

I leaned way out, grabbed the bar of the door, and pulled. The door slammed shut, leaving me and Davy alone again in the dim, ghostly light of the exit signs as the thing outside pounded wetly on the side of the funhouse.

Davy was standing now, looking around from one mirror to another. They all looked the same to me, but he grabbed my arm and said, "Come on." Then he frowned and looked at me. "Are you okay? You're bleeding."

Now that he mentioned it, my lip still hurt, and there was a chunk torn out and it was still bleeding. I had forgotten about that while we were running. "I'll be okay. Which way did we come in?"

Davy looked around again and said, "I don't know, but let's move."

"Wait," I said. I remembered something. "Put one hand on the wall and keep it there and keep walking. You can always get out of a maze that way."

Davy frowned. "I don't think that works."

"Of course it does," I said.

He shook his head. "It only works in certain kinds of mazes."

"Just do it," I said. "You're smart, but you don't know everything."

Davy looked hurt for a second, but then he turned and touched a mirror with his right hand and started walking.

I touched the mirror and followed. We wound around from one mirror to the next, turning left and right and right and left, for what seemed like a long time.

"Crapola," Davy said. "Look."

We were back at the side door where we were going to jump out before. The zombie wasn't pounding on the door anymore. Davy and I looked at each other. He looked scared. I bet I did, too.

I said, "Maybe we did it wrong."

He shook his head. "I never took my hand off the mirrors. Did you?"

"No. Look, Davy, I'm sorry about what I said. I thought—"

"Wrong kind of maze," he said. "Not your fault."

I was all turned around now. I didn't know which way was which. Except for the exit signs being reversed in some of the mirrors, I couldn't tell one from another. "What are you supposed to do with this kind of maze?"

"You're supposed to get lost."

Somewhere not too far away, something grunted.

Davy said, "Are you still bleeding?"

I poked at the gash in my lip with my tongue and tasted blood. I nodded.

"Let's do the one hand thing on the other side," he said. "But smear a little blood on each mirror. If we find one with blood on it, it means we've been there. So we switch to the other side."

We each put our left hands on a mirror. I swabbed in my mouth with a finger and dabbed a little bit of blood on the mirror at chin height. In the icy blue light the blood didn't look red. It looked black. Like zombie blood.

Something moved. It wasn't me or Davy, but something flashed from two or three of the mirrors.

"Let's move," Davy said, and started forward, his left hand dragging along the mirror.

As we walked, I dabbed blood on each mirror. I smeared the sixth mirror, then squinted at it. The smear wasn't as black as it had been. It was mostly just spit.

"What are you waiting for," Davy said. "Zombies?"

"I'm not bleeding any more."

Davy looked down at his T-shirt, then at my shirt. He pointed. "Your buttons. Drop a button next to each mirror. And when you run out, I'll drop my shoes and socks. Then you can drop yours. We'll drop our pants if we have to."

At any other time, that would have been funny. But I had another idea. "Hold on," I said, holding up a finger. I pressed my thumb below my lip so that the flapping chunk was hanging over my bottom teeth. Then I bit hard, and the chunk fell onto my tongue. The pain brought tears to my eyes and I couldn't see for a second. But I tasted blood. Plenty of blood.

I kept my lips closed, but poked my finger in. It came out black. I smeared the mirror.

In the mirrors, something moved, still shapeless but bigger now, dark and jerky. I heard a wet sniff, but I couldn't tell what direction. The smell had changed, deepened, something like pee after you've eaten asparagus, but moldy and rotting.

The thing in the mirror maze made a low-pitched moaning sound, then chuckled.

"Let's go," I said, and Davy started moving again.

I kept smearing the mirrors as we passed. Twice we ended up at a smeared mirror, and had to switch to another one where we hadn't been yet.

We turned a corner and saw the zombie's face right in front of us, but it was smaller than in real life. The zombie sprang forward. Its face hit a mirror and its head bounced back. It pounded on the mirror with its fists and yelled, a flapping gurgling sound. Then it reached out, wiped a finger down the mirror, and touched the finger to its grey-blue tongue.

"It found your blood," Davy said. "We have to switch."

I didn't really want to turn around, to show my back to the thing, but I did. I put my left hand out, smeared the mirror with my right hand, and stepped forward around a corner.

There, six feet in front of me, was the entrance door. A sign, barely visible in the dim light, read SCAREDY CAT EXIT.

The door opened with a blast of sunlight. Silhouetted in the doorway was a tall man-shaped thing. One hand rested on the door frame. Its other hand—well, it had no other hand. It's other arm ended in a puckered stump.

Somewhere behind Davy, the zombie that had eaten Kippy chuckled again.

Davy stepped up beside me and pushed me sideways. I stumbled between some mirrors on one side and he ducked between on the other side. "We should split up."

"No way," I said.

"At least one of us has to get to the zoo, get the shotguns."

"Okay."

My eyes were adjusting to the sunlight. The zombie in the doorway tsuk tsukked its tongue. A heavy bump shook the wall behind me and I turned around. Kippy's zombie was sniffing the air and looking at us.

I looked back and forth from one zombie to the other. They looked back and forth from Davy to me.

"Try to keep them in a mirror," Davy said. "It's safer if you see a reversed exit sign over their heads."

"Braaaains," the zombie in the door said, and looked at Davy.

"Brrrrainss," Kippy's zombie said, and looked at Davy.

Davy turned and ran, and so did I.

I ran smack into a mirror hard enough to make sparks fly in my head and knock me to my knees. This was a dead end. There was nothing to do but wait for the zombies to get me.

I turned my head in time to see both zombies turn away from me and disappear around the corner where Davy had gone.

Davy said, "Go, Markie, go. Get the shotguns."

Then he started screaming.

I jumped up and ran toward the scaredy cat exit, toward the sunlight.

And speaking of smarter, Davy was right about the zoo. They must have had shotguns for if animals escaped. And rifles, too. By the time I got to the entrance, there were about a dozen people guarding the way in. The animals were all going crazy and shrieking and jumping around. Even the two enormous, squat hippos were running around and jumping, smashing the watermelons and cabbages that they should have been eating.

So I sat on a stone bench in the zoo while the men blasted away at any zombie who came near. And in my head I kept hearing Davy. Not screaming, thank God. I kept hearing him tell me to keep the exit signs reversed over the zombies' heads.

No zombies got into the zoo. I was safe there. Safe and ashamed.

Yes, I ran. I acted like a coward. But that's not what I'm ashamed of. As horrible as it is to say it, by the time I ran, it was too late for Davy. You can judge me if you want, but you would have run, too, if you had been in that funhouse that day.

No, what I'm ashamed of is that my little brother was smarter than me. He was always smarter, and that's why it was him that died. If I had been smarter, that zombie would have come after me instead.

For the rest of the summer I'm going to read school books. I'm going to study real hard. I'm going to be smarter, as smart as I can be, even though I know I'll never be as smart as Davy. I know, you're probably thinking how stupid that sounds. Ha ha. Well, I know that. I know it won't change anything. I know it's too late to save Davy. But it's all I've got to hold onto.

Author's Note

Once upon a time in a dark corner of the blogosphere, June 13 was known as Blog Like It's The End Of The World Day (BLITEOTW). On that day, people from all over the world would blog about the zombie apocalypse in real time.

I participated in 2008. I wrote about zombie goats in my back yard. This marked the second time I wrote about zombie goats. The first will likely never see the light of day. I have a super-duper-top-secret reason for writing about zombie goats. But it's on a need to know basis.

I also wrote about zombie squirrels. My reasons for that are a secret for which even I have insufficient clearance.

A few weeks after my first Blog Like It's The End Of The World Day, the idea for Funhouse *popped into my head. The whole thing. Beginning, middle, and end. I even knew the exact location of the funhouse. I didn't know all of the details, but I knew the gist of the whole story.*

I planned to write it for BLITEOTW Day 2009.

2009 came and went. Then 2010. And 2011. You can guess how this progression progresses. I didn't write it. I don't know why.

By now you will be sensing a pattern in my writing process. I get an idea, then set it aside for years. Then I pick up the idea, start typing, and quickly finish the story. It's not as if I figure out how to write the stories in the interim. None of these stories "percolated." Each time I resumed a story, I had no more clue of the story than when I'd set it aside.

So here is what gets the story finished: I start typing. That's it. It's no more magical than that. And no less magical. When the writer is ready, the story will appear. And "ready" means "typing."

I was surprised that the story ended up at about 3,000 words. I expected 1,500 or so. Getting those kids out of that funhouse was harder than I expected. Sorry, Davy. Sorry, Kippy.

Let me issue the standard fiction disclaimer here. These characters are fictional. Yes, I do have a little brother named Davy. And yes, Davy had a boyhood friend named Kippy. But neither of them is in this story. Honest.

Here is my evidence: First, Davy and Kippy grew up in Maine. That's way different from Sacramento. Second, and probably more important, neither Davy nor Kippy has ever been eaten by a zombie. Not once.

Not yet.

YANTRIEL'S PRIVY

1. A Pig or a Daughter

GARNO STRODE THROUGH MY FRONT DOOR, took one look at me, and said, "This is the last free one, Yantriel. The next time will cost you either a pig or a daughter."

He smiled in that oily way he has, all on one side, one eyebrow jutting up and one corner of his mouth pulling back. He tilted his head and the peak of his pointed blue silk hat flopped over one eyebrow. He ran his thumbs up the lapels of his gold-embroidered blue silk jacket and bounced on the balls of his feet. The blue of his jacket was about four shades lighter and three shades greener than the blue of his hat. And the gold embroidery was frayed and dingy.

A pig or a daughter. That's what he said last time. But when I called his bluff and offered him my eldest daughter—Clambeth, the smart one—he just shook his head and mumbled. And I wasn't about to offer him a pig. He was bluffing about the daughter—I was pretty confident about that—but he might take me up on a pig. I couldn't afford to give up a whole pig no matter how much I needed him.

And I needed him. By now, the frogs crawling out of my outhouse covered most of the hill behind the barn.

And not just any old frogs. These were smart frogs. You get enough of these smart frogs together in one place—the hill behind my barn, say—and they'll outsmart your average farmer.

They had me flummoxed, that's for sure.

They crawled all over each other, a squirming, yellow-green mass of fist-sized frogs. They formed a low heap about thirty feet across and three feet thick at the middle.

Now, I ain't exactly squeamish. As any farmer will tell you, a squeamish farmer is an ex-farmer. But I got to admit, these frogs gave me the creeps. Not the squirming. That weren't it. And not the sheer mass of them, neither. No, what gave me the creeps was the eyes. Almost human, them eyes. They look right at you like they see right inside you. Like they know all your secrets. Intelligent eyes. Big, warm, brown eyes.

Like my dear, late wife's eyes, may she rest in peace.

I probably hadn't ought to admit that, comparing these hideous frogs' eyes to my lovely Paelene's. But true is true.

You might well ask, if the frogs are so darned smart, why do they make their entrance into this world through an outhouse? And in particular, why my outhouse?

Well, they may be smart, but they ain't talking. Not so far, at least.

Now, smart is a relative thing. But I mean these frogs are smart. Let me give you an example.

A few years ago two raccoons got into the outhouse. They didn't do any real damage, but they were down in the hole at sunrise when Clambeth settled in for her morning constitutional. Not two minutes later Paelene and I heard an awful racket—two or three kinds of screams all mixed up together. We ran out the back door just as Clambeth and them two coons shot out the privy door in three separate directions. I can't say who got the worst of it, but we never saw those coons again.

At any rate, Clambeth and me rigged up a latch on that door to keep the critters out. I say Clambeth and me. At first I tried to do it myself, but I ain't mechanically minded. The latch worked well enough, such as it was. I stepped out of the privy, closed the door, and heard the latch make a satisfying little clunk.

Then I realized my mistake. I was outside. The latch was inside.

Okay, so maybe I ain't the best guy to judge intelligence.

After I pulled that door down with a crowbar, I drug Clambeth out of the house to help me. She was reluctant to revisit the scene of her morning excitement, but she understood the need well enough. Clambeth is the smart one in the family. We poked a latch through a hole in the wall up above eye level, and pivoted it on a little rocker, so you could open it from inside or out, if you were tall enough. We upended a slop bucket outside the door so little Pegnel could reach it. To look up at her now, you wouldn't suppose Pegnel ever had trouble reaching the latch, or the weather vane we stuck up on the outhouse roof as a joke, for that matter. But she weren't quite so tall back then.

Clambeth and me were pretty sure that if the raccoons were ever brave enough to waddle back for another adventure, they wouldn't be able to reach the latch. Even if they climbed up on the bucket. Of course, that was all speculation. As far as I know, they never came back.

Them frogs, on the other hand. They figured out the latch right away, on the very first night they crawled up out of the hole.

As for their first appearance, three weeks ago, the day of the summer solstice, all I can say is I'm glad I was the first one to wander out back that morning. The raccoon adventure two years before had spooked Clambeth so bad that for more than a month she wouldn't even go out the back door by herself, much less all the way to the outhouse, latch or no latch.

But what if she'd been the one to reach for the privy latch that solstice morning instead of me? What if that latch had flipped, seemingly of its own accord, inches from her hand instead of mine? What if that enormous wave of yellow-green, fist-sized, brown-eyed frogs had spilled out the door onto her bare feet instead of mine? There's no telling when she'd ever be regular again.

Clambeth is a little skittish, sure. But she is the smart one of the family. Garno would be lucky to have her.

And now here he was standing in my entryway, his ridiculous blue silk hat flopped over toward his left eyebrow, swearing that this was the last time he'd fix my little frog problem without some kind of substantial remuneration. The fleshy kind.

Last time he'd said that, I didn't know just how bad I needed him. This time I knew. I'd be more than happy to give him his choice of my pigs.

"Fair enough," I said. "There's a lot more of them this time."

"Pigs, or daughters?" he said. He glanced over my shoulder at the girls. Specifically at Pegnel, from the upward angle of his gaze. I think he'd have licked his lips if he hadn't been within arm's reach.

"Frogs," I said.

I took him around the house instead of through. I didn't want him anywhere near my youngest. Clambeth, she'd be sharp enough to set him straight if he needed straightening. Or any man, for that matter, which is probably why she's still living under my roof. But Pegnel, she may be taller than most grown women, and many grown men, for that matter. But she's still young in most ways.

As we rounded the corner of the house, Garno stopped short and let out a slow whistle. "A lot more of them."

I nodded. "Like I said."

"If this keeps up, I might have to raise my price."

That started me wondering. When the frogs had come back after Garno "dispatched" them the first time, he had seemed surprised. And after he dispatched them again, and five days later I informed him that the frogs had come back yet again, he seemed not only surprised but genuinely dismayed. But a lot of things, and a lot of people, seem what they ain't. Could he have been playacting in order to extract a price? Most likely not. Not that I would trust him as far as I could fling a hog. But I known him a long time, and I don't think he'd do me like that. And yet.

He must have seen my thoughts on my face, because he held up a placating hand and said, "I'm joking, Yantriel. This situation is most puzzling. But I assure you I'll do everything in my power."

I didn't understand his power. I suspect he didn't either. He called it animal magnetism, but it seemed to me more like animal repulsion. If you had a problem with a coyote or a bobcat poking around your sheep or goats, you'd call Garno and he'd get rid of it. He would do something—he never let his clients see what it was—and the animal in question would never, ever be seen again. Nobody knew where they went. Not even Garno, if you believe him. But it was like they'd been removed from creation. Like magic.

And it worked every time. Up until the frogs.

"I'm confident," Garno said, "that the frogs I dispatched on the previous two occasions will never come back." He tilted his head and scratched his ear the way he does. "But these are not the same frogs."

"All the same kind, though. Look at them eyes. No earthly frogs have eyes like that."

"Sadly, I can dispatch only specific individuals. I do not know how to dispatch a kind. And I have been reluctant to experiment, given the delicate balances of nature."

"Do you have to see individual animals? Be within a certain distance?"

"No. I just have to see them in my mind's eye."

That didn't make sense to me, how he could dispatch an individual animal without seeing the exact animal he was dispatching. But it made sense to him. And it worked. That was what mattered. "Then why not dispatch all of the individuals? Every single one?"

Garno's eyes came kinda unfocused and he stared off into the distance for a long time. Then he blinked and looked at me. "What a brilliant idea."

I felt pretty good about that. Garno don't give out compliments easy. And just maybe I'd figured a way to finally get rid of them frogs once and for durn tooting.

Then he shooed me away, saying he'd holler in an hour or so, after he'd dispatched the frogs.

That good feeling lasted through the half dozen games of Cobblestones I played with my daughters at the kitchen table. Clambeth won all but one, and I suspect she let Pegnel win that one.

Then Clambeth said, "How long did Garno say he would be?"

And just like that the good feeling was gone.

We all shoved our chairs back and ran out the back door.

Pegnel shouted and pointed at the hill behind the barn. "Father, look. The frogs."

The frogs were gone. I couldn't see a one. I also couldn't see any of the grass that had covered the hill before the frogs came. That was a shame. But the frogs were gone.

And Garno was gone, too.

Maybe he had finished up and gone home, but that weren't like him. Whenever he finished a job, he liked to show off his handiwork and get a pat on the back.

I was concerned that he weren't there. But mostly I wanted to ask if he'd been able to dispatch the rest of the frogs. The rest of their kind.

The outhouse door waved back and forth in the breeze, squeaking gently in each direction. I was pretty sure the door had been closed when Garno shooed me away. Maybe he checked in there to make sure he dispatched all of the frogs.

But it didn't feel right, that door swinging back and forth like that.

"You stay right here," I said to the girls, as sternly as I could. Then I walked down to the outhouse, trying not to let them see my nerves.

Garno weren't inside. I started to back out and close the door when I saw a flash of something through the privy hole. I stepped in and looked down.

There was Garno's ridiculous blue silk hat, hanging on a nail about halfway down the wall of the pit. Further down, all the way at the bottom, were the rest of Garno's clothes.

But no sign of Garno.

I heard the girls step up behind me, one on either side of the door. Clambeth said, "What is it, Papa? Where's Garno?"

"I sure hope he got them all," I said, leaving her second question unanswered for now. But inside, I didn't have much hope at all.

2. The Slop Bucket

OF COURSE THE FROGS CAME BACK. Of course they did. Four days later. Right up out of the privy, just like they done three times before. I never did figure out how they got up the privy pit walls. Maybe they had sticky feet. I was afraid to touch them to find out. Afraid to get within ten feet of them, for that matter. It was the eyes.

We spotted the frogs early this time, Clambeth and Pegnel and me. We kept watch around the clock. I propped the outhouse door open with a stick, and we set up a stool about twenty yards east of the outhouse. With the door open, twenty yards weren't quite enough distance for comfort in a westerly breeze. And on top of the smell, the late July humidity made the foul breeze thick and slow. And humid. Let's just say we were committed to noticing those frogs the very moment they came back.

Not that we had the slightest idea what we was going to do about them when they did come. Garno had been our only hope of getting rid of them. I should have been more generous with that man.

It was Pegnel that saw the first one, about two hours before dawn. Her screaming woke me up from a fitful sleep. She swears she never screamed. "I called for you in a loud, determined voice," she says. I don't fault her for screaming. Or for denying it.

I ran down the stairs, fumbling with my shaking hands to get my nightclothes wrapped around me decent. By the time

I got out the door, Clambeth had already reached Pegnel. She was holding onto her younger sister, who was bent over far enough to put her head into Clambeth's shoulder.

"One of us should probably go look in there," Clambeth said.

I stroked my chin in what I hoped was a thoughtful manner. Maybe a better idea would come, if I gave myself a minute to wake up.

"Before more of them come out," Clambeth said. The moon was only a crescent, but that was enough for me to see the glare in her eyes. Her blue eyes. She looked nothing like her mother. But in sixteen years she had picked up her mother's talent for expressing an imperative without saying a word. And with a certain amount of urgency.

In my haste on the way out of the house I had neglected to pick up a lantern. I pointed to the one Pegnel clutched in one white-knuckled hand. She looked down at it, then back up at me, her eyes wide and wet. She let go of Clambeth and gripped the lantern in both hands, pulling it a little closer. For a long minute I didn't think she was going to hand it over, but then she did, albeit very slowly.

There was nothing left to do now but get on with it. So I did. Albeit very slowly.

I felt like a coward every step of the way, wanting to turn back, grab my two daughters in my arms, load everything up into a wagon, and run. Abandon the farm that had been in my family for three hundred years and run. But all I could see in my mind's eye was them two beautiful girls never quite looking their father square in the eye again. So on I went.

As I approached, I could see four frogs sitting on the bench of the privy, one at each point of the compass, just at the edge of the hole.

I stopped outside the outhouse door to pick up that bucket I'd set down years before, the one Pegnel had long since stopped using as a step stool. By the time I looked back through the door there were six frogs, equally spaced in a tidy circle around the privy hole. Twelve big brown eyes staring at me unblinking in the lantern light.

With some effort I lifted one foot and stepped forward, ever so tentative. As my foot came gently to rest on the doorstep, them frogs scattered, all at once, each in a different direction.

Now, look. When I say they went different directions, that don't tell the half of it. Not directly away from me, like you might expect from regular frogs. And not in random directions. They spread out, straight from the center of that privy hole, making their circle wider.

And scattered ain't the right word either. Scattered might suggest panic, or at least fear. I don't think these frogs had a lick of fear in them. Each one of them frogs took but a single hop. A deliberate hop. A well-considered hop, if I judged it right.

Then every one of them frogs turned right straight toward me, as if they was waiting to see what I would do next.

I slowly brought my other foot up alongside the first. When it set down gently on the doorstep, every blessed one of them six frogs turned and took one deliberate hop outward. Two of them flew off the edge of the bench and landed with wet plops on the floor to either side of the door. Then, just as they had done before, them frogs all turned toward me.

I swear they was acting just like a pack of dogs, almost inviting me toward the spot they was clearing in between them.

Now the question was which frog I was going to try to drop the bucket onto. As for what I would do with the thing once I had it in the bucket, I left that problem to be pondered on a subsequent occasion.

The two on the floor were out of the question. I'd have to bend over to get at them, and that meant turning my back to the others. That weren't going to happen if I could help it. And I had come to regret rushing out of the house without putting on my boots.

I decided I'd go for the one nearest to me, to the left of the hole. I upended the bucket, lifted my right foot and—very, very slowly—eased it forward to the edge of the bench.

The frogs didn't move. They watched.

I eased the bucket out in front of me, about a foot over the frog, and began to lower it ever so slowly.

The frog below the bucket didn't move.

Then the bucket was low enough that I couldn't see the frog.

"Got you!" I shouted, and slammed the bucket down.

At that very instant, something wet landed on my bare left foot.

I screamed and jumped back, shaking my foot and flailing my hands. The edge of the bucket hit me square on the right eyebrow. The frog flew off my foot and thumped against the wall and landed on its back. It righted itself with a jerk of its hind legs, then hopped. Once. Right back to the spot where it had been.

Not one of the other frogs had moved. Not even the one I'd nearly trapped under the bucket. Not so much as an inch.

My foot felt cool from whatever slime the frog had shed on it. And whatever filth it had collected as it crawled up from the pit.

But there was no burning or itching or numbness or whatever else I might have feared would ooze out of these unearthly abominations. Just cool.

I found that surprisingly comforting.

I raised up my bucket again. If one of them floor frogs jumped on my foot again, so be it. And I watched the others out of the corner of my eye. I promised myself I would not flinch if they jumped.

I lowered the bucket again. This time I didn't slam it, or shout a warning. I just lowered it inch by inch. If that frog was stupid enough to just sit there, that would be fine by me.

Now a regular frog, once you get the bucket down low enough, can't jump away. If it jumps at all, which they nearly always do, it will jump right up into the bucket.

That's where the bucket was.

And the frog rolled out from underneath.

Frogs don't roll. They lack the musculature for it. Ain't got the skeletal structure. But this frog rolled away like a person might if something was falling on them. Rolled over and over until it was about two feet away, next to the wall.

Then it turned and looked at me.

I looked at each one of them frogs, one after the other. Looked them right in the eyes. What I was looking for, I can't say exactly. Some sign of fear or vulnerability.

What I saw instead was dead calm. As if they knew they were defeating me.

Well, I wasn't done just yet.

But one thing was for sure. That slop bucket weren't going to get the job done. I was going to need heavier artillery.

3. Unnerving Fidelity

CLAMBETH KEPT AN EYE ON THE OUTHOUSE. Pegnel and me rummaged around the barn and cobbled together two smoke pots out of clay jars and burlap and lamp oil. The outhouse weren't exactly airtight, but I guessed it would hold the smoke in long enough to make breathing problematical for the frogs. Assuming they breathed.

"Hurry, Papa," Clambeth shouted. Morning was dawning in the east.

Pegnel and me lugged the two clay pots, now stuffed to overflowing with oiled burlap, out to the stool where Clambeth sat, her eyes fixed on the frogs twenty yards away.

Clambeth pointed. "There are three more now."

I waited with Pegnel while Clambeth ran off to the house to fetch the tinderbox and a torch.

"I'm sorry about Garno," Pegnel said. "About what happened to him."

"I feel kinda bad about it, myself," I said. Truth be told, I felt more than a little bad about it.

"I think he liked me."

"Of course he did," I said. Then I realized what she was saying. "What do you mean?"

"I liked him, too."

Before I could inquire further about what sort of relationship Garno and my fourteen-year-old daughter might have developed while I weren't paying attention, Clambeth rounded the corner of the house with a torch in one hand and the tinderbox under the other arm.

Three or four more frogs had emerged at the top of the privy seat. There were a dozen or more now, crowded close together, watching the girls and me with what appeared for all the world to be curiosity.

"You two light the torch," I said, "then I'll light the smoke pots and drop them down the hole."

Pegnel held the torch and Clambeth struck the flint. The torch caught a spark and in a moment was ablaze. I tucked the two clay jars under one arm, and Clambeth handed me the torch.

"We make a pretty good team," I said. "Now you girls stay right here. I don't mind saying I got no idea what's going to happen."

Clambeth nodded. Pegnel frowned. I turned toward the outhouse.

The number of frogs had doubled while we were lighting the torch.

It was time to put an end to this. I took a step forward.

One of the frogs hopped off the bench and landed on the stick I'd used to prop open the outhouse door. The stick didn't budge and the frog tumbled over it onto the ground. It would have been comical if I hadn't been so darned scared.

Then the frog jumped straight up and hit the stick full-bodied from underneath. The stick broke in half and the door began to swing shut in the breeze. The frog took one hop to the edge of the doorway, then jumped straight up again, just as the door was about to bang against the outhouse.

The frog was too late. The door caught it in the midsection, its hind legs spasming as the door trapped it against the doorjamb.

Got one, I thought.

Then—and I swear to you it happened just this way—two frog hands reached down from inside, grabbed that dangling frog by one hind leg, and pulled it up.

And now I couldn't see what was happening inside. Couldn't see what kind of plans they was making. What kind of defenses they was arranging.

If I could get in there with these smoke pots, I was pretty sure these frogs wouldn't have no defenses against that. The thing was, I couldn't be absolutely sure.

As I approached the outhouse I found that I had no free hands to open the door. I thought to call one of the girls over, but I didn't want them anywhere near these frogs. So I lifted one foot, curled my toes around the edge of the door, and swung it open.

And there on the privy sat Garno.

Except that it weren't Garno at all. It was a writhing mass of frogs all clung together in a sickening, Garno-shaped mass. And it was wearing Garno's blue silk hat and incompatibly blue silk jacket, both of them now filthy. The hat flopped down over its— Well, I'll call it a face, and leave it at that.

Behind me, in a tiny, girlish voice, Pegnel said, "Garno?"

"You stay back," I shouted. I wanted to turn around and reinforce the command with a stern fatherly look, but no way was I going to take my eyes off of them frogs.

I let one smoke pot slide down to my hand and hooked a thumb over the rim. I held the torch between me and the frogs and bent my knees slowly to lower the pot to the ground in front of me. The firelight glinted off what must have been a hundred eyes.

The frog mass's hands—now, you realize that hands ain't the right word, but I don't know how else to give you a clear picture of what I was seeing—its hands slid up its chest, mimicking Garno's pompous lapel stroking with unnerving fidelity.

I slid the other pot down to my hand and stepped forward.

"Father," Pegnel said.

"Stay back," I said again. "Do you hear me?"

"Father, I love him."

That stopped me in my tracks.

I wanted to spin around, march right back to where Pegnel was standing, shake her by the shoulders, and demand that she tell me exactly what a fourteen-year-old girl thought she knew about love. And how she'd fallen in with this man who was well beyond twice her years, not to mention dead. And all without me having a hint of a suspicion of a clue.

"It ain't him," I said, shaking my head.

The frog mass tilted its head and smiled. One frog, clutching onto the front of the face, arched its spine, imitating the jut of Garno's eyebrow. Another, lower down the face, arched sideways in a grotesque caricature of the corner of a lip pulling back.

"You don't know that," Pegnel said. "Not for sure."

As soon as she said it, I realized she was right. I didn't know it. I didn't know that this squirming mass of slimy green creatures wasn't Garno. Maybe they had eaten him, or incorporated him into them somehow. I didn't know.

My next thought sent a chill through me like I've never known.

I didn't know—not for sure—that them eyes weren't Paelene's.

I wanted to bury that thought as far down in the pit of my mind as I could.

I blinked. Hard. So hard that my eyes blurred. So I can't say for sure that this next thing actually happened.

What I saw—or thought I saw—was the frog mass shrinking ever so slightly. Its shoulders rounding, tilting forward. And the frogs around the face puffing outward to the sides, their webbed hands and feet swinging out gently, swaying. Just the way Paelene's hair used to do.

"Father, please," Pegnel said.

And I'm ever grateful that she did.

Her words broke my reverie. Paelene was gone. Pegnel and Clambeth were my world now.

I held the torch in front of me and stepped forward with a purpose.

"Let me go!" Pegnel screamed.

Good girl, Clambeth.

In one sloppy motion, the frog mass collapsed into itself and splutted straight down the privy hole. The frogs held onto each other and the leg masses swung out, then up, then followed the body down the hole.

I tilted the clay pot and touched the torch flame to the oily burlap that flapped out the top. The pot flared into flame and I dropped it down the hole. It left an oily black trail of smoke as it fell.

Pegnel screamed.

"Papa!" Clambeth shouted.

Down below I heard scores of thumps as the frogs tried to escape the smoke.

I grabbed the privy lid and slammed it down.

As I turned to reach for the second smoke pot, Pegnel hit me at a dead run and knocked me back onto the privy lid with a thud.

And she made to come at me again.

I lifted one leg and turned sideways so that if she hit me it wouldn't hurt neither of us too bad.

But at the last minute she stopped and she screamed. Her eyes went wide, her gaze fixed over my shoulder.

I'd set the wall of the privy afire.

"Get the fire buckets!" I shouted to Clambeth. I figured it wouldn't do no good to give Pegnel orders just then.

But Clambeth stepped into view behind Pegnel. "Better to let it burn, Papa. And best to help it along." She held up the second smoke pot.

Clambeth always was the smart one of the family. Either that or she'd plain had enough of that privy for one lifetime.

"Father, no," Pegnel said. But it didn't sound like she was saying not to do it. More like she was saying no to the world. To the weird grief of what was happening. Trying not to accept that it weren't Garno down in the hole after all.

"Step back a ways, darling," I said, and she did.

Clambeth handed me the smoke pot.

I lit it and handed the torch to her. "You step back, too." The greasy, acrid smoke began to fill up the outhouse.

Clambeth took a half step back and nodded. "Hurry, Papa."

I opened the privy lid just barely wide enough, then slipped the pot through and let it fall.

The lid was open for just a second. Just long enough to hear rapid fire thumping against the walls of the pit. And just long enough to hear one more sound that I will never forget.

Paelene's sweet voice, calling gently up out of the hole. Just one word.

"Yantriel," the voice said.

I dropped the lid and touched the torch all around the outhouse.

Clambeth and Pegnel and I backed five paces away as the fire and smoke consumed the privy.

Arm in arm, we watched for a very long time.

4. Chilly Winter

WE KEPT THE FIRE BURNING for three solid weeks, dropping in another stick of our best hardwood whenever the coals started to burn down.

When everything had burned that was likely to burn, we lined the pit with tar and filled it in with rocks and mortar. I'm confident that the three of us are now the proud owners of the least destructible former privy hole anyone in these parts has ever seen.

We dug the new privy on the other side of the house, on the edge of an embankment, so that the back of the pit would be more accessible by shovel. And to make it less accessible by frog—you see, we can't be sure the frogs are gone for good, and we darned well ain't taking any chances—we lined the pit walls with three sheets of iron, with thick layers of mortar in between. And a thick steel door with heavy hinges and four steel rods to bar it closed. That was Clambeth's idea.

So far we've got through one winter without seeing frog one. But was that due to the thoroughness of our construction work? And our destruction work? Or was it just the cold weather?

We'll know soon enough. The equinox is three weeks behind us, and the weather is starting to warm up.

And Pegnel is warming up again. The winter was a chilly one between us. As the days passed, I became less and less interested in learning just what had happened between her and Garno. But she will talk to me from time to time, and join Clambeth and me for a game or two of Cobblestones. The one thing she ain't done is offered any conversation about Garno. And I ain't asked.

I think it's going to be that way for a long, long time.

But we're all right, the girls and me. As right as we can be.

Author's Note

Like Tailor's Tears, Yantriel's Privy *began as nothing more than a first line.*

One day in 2013 I decided to analyze the first lines of mystery, science fiction, and fantasy stories. I grabbed the latest issues of Asimov's Science Fiction *magazine,* The Magazine of Fantasy and Science Fiction, Alfred Hitchcock's Mystery Magazine, *and* Ellery Queen's Mystery Magazine. *I also grabbed the 2011 and 2012 volumes of* America's Best Mystery Stories.

I opened a Scrivener file and typed the first line of every story. Dozens and dozens of stories. Then, one by one, I asked: What is going on in this opening line?

I began to notice common patterns in the opening lines. Someone arriving. Going to a meeting, or preparing for a meeting. A description of the status quo, soon to be interrupted. A storyteller launching into an obvious tall tale. Someone reminiscing about someone they knew long ago. I noticed more than a dozen patterns.

Then, for each pattern, I wrote two or three opening lines of my own.

For the "someone arriving" pattern, my third opening line was:

> Garno strode through the door, took one look at me, and said, "This is the last free one, Yantriel. The next one will cost you either a pig or a daughter."

Well, that amused me. As usual—and you will have detected

the pattern yourself by now—I had no clue what the story was. No clue what who Yantriel or Garno were. No clue what Yantriel's problem was, what sort of help Garno offered, or why the problem kept coming back.

So I began typing.

A page into the story, I discovered the problem: Yantriel's outhouse was overflowing the frogs.

Oh, no.

I couldn't write a story about frogs overflowing an outhouse. That would be just too silly.

I almost set the story aside to brainstorm other ideas for what Yantriel's problem might be. Almost.

But Yantriel kept telling the story.

And I noticed that Yantriel was regaling me in a Maine accent. Not one of those gawdawful Hollywood Maine accents that every lazy-assed actor seems to have learned from Tom Bosley. A real, honest to goodness, downeast, ayuh Maine accent.

I grew up in Maine. My grandparents, who lived in the farm across the road from ours, had an outhouse. A two-holer. Very friendly. For sharing. And another neighbor also had an outhouse. One time, at a party at the neighbor's house, a woman got her head stuck in the privy hole. I wish I knew the story behind that. (Surely there's a story.)

But this I do know: Outhouses are fun. Maine accents are fun. And as early as page two, this story had both an outhouse and a Maine accent. Oh, and frogs. Frogs that, as I was about to find out, were no ordinary frogs.

How could I resist that?

So I kept typing.

As I was writing this story, I stopped frequently to read it out loud. I also giggled a lot. In a Maine accent.

About the Author

DALE HARTLEY EMERY writes fiction in a variety of genres, including fantasy, science fiction, and mystery. His short stories include *Carrion Road*, *Yantriel's Privy*, and *The Last Whiskey Bacon Cheddar Burger at Saint Florian's Abbey*.

Dale has worked as a failed shoemaker, reluctant dairy farmer, and ruthless ice cream man. For several years he monitored the nuclear test ban treaty, making sure those pesky commies didn't blow up the planet. (They didn't.)

When he isn't writing, Dale advises software teams and leaders about how to play nice together. Colleagues in Dale's industry once created a special award for him for being reasonable.

Dale lives in California with his wife.

CONNECT
WITH DALE HARTLEY EMERY

WEBSITE
http://DaleHartleyEmery.com

FACEBOOK
http://facebook.com/DaleHartleyEmery

GOODREADS
http://goodreads.com/DaleHartleyEmery

GOOGLE+
https://google.com/+DaleHartleyEmeryWriter

TWITTER
http://twitter.com/dalewriting

Books by Dale Hartley Emery

Science Fiction and Fantasy

Carrion Road

Funhouse

Refund

Tailor's Tears

Yantriel's Privy

Collections

Winding Unwinding

For more information about these books
and other fine fiction from Driscoll Brook Press,
visit www.DriscollBrookPress.com

www.ingramcontent.com/pod-product-compliance
Lightning Source LLC
Chambersburg PA
CBHW022033170626
46808CB00003B/1177